A Christmas Bride

A Christmas Bride

JO ANN FERGUSON

OPEN ROAD

INTEGRATED MEDIA

NEW YORK

Cover design by Julianna Lee

ISBN: 978-1-5040-5328-0

This edition published in 2018 by Open Road Integrated Media, Inc.
180 Maiden Lane
New York, NY 10038
www.openroadmedia.com

For Robin,

You have taught me many things
—and I thank you for all of them.
But most of all I thank you for your friendship.

A Christmas Bride

ONE

"All we need to do is find you a fiancée by tomorrow."

Timothy Crawford ignored his cousin's laugh. This was no laughing matter, and Felix should be quite aware of that. He thought that they had been in each other's pockets for long enough that his cousin would appreciate the gravity of this situation. This was all his own doing. If he had been honest with his grandfather, he would not be suffering from this predicament now.

Putting his glass on the table by the chair in his dimly lit parlor, Timothy rose and went to the window to look out on the square that was almost lost in the London fog. He clasped his hands behind his back to keep them from curling into fists of frustration.

What a bumble-bath! He had wanted only to ease his grandfather's anxiety about future heirs. When he had devised the story of a wondrous woman who had agreed to be his wife, he had not guessed he would actually have to produce her for his grandfather's inspection at his seventieth birthday celebration on Christmas Eve.

"How difficult can it be?" Felix continued, splashing more wine into his glass as he came to stand beside Timothy. He was half a head shorter, and, instead of the golden hair that was the hallmark of their family, his hair was a dull brown. "You are a viscount with our grandfather's title of earl to be yours upon his death. Cheyney Park is a magnificent country seat, and you shall have enough blunt to satisfy even the most demanding wife. I am sure, with no more than a crook of your finger, you shall be able to find any number of lasses eager to betroth themselves to you."

"I have plied Grandfather with out-and-outers for too long." He sighed. "I have no choice but to be honest." He reached for his glass and raised it to his lips, but it was empty.

Felix obligingly refilled it. "He will disown you. You shall have the title, but not a copper penny to go along with it."

"Which will be your father's good fortune, for he would be next to inherit it." He rubbed his eyes. How long had it been since he last slept? Two days? Three? He was not sure of the number of days, but knew it had been since the letter had arrived from Cheyney Park with the request that Timothy and his fiancée, Serenity Adams, attend the earl's birthday celebration.

Serenity Adams! He wished he never had written to his grandfather of this paragon of femininity. No woman he had met during the Season here in Town matched her perfection, with her ebony hair and silver-blue eyes. He had even gone so far as to describe in his letters to his grandfather how she was a pattern-card of style, favoring bright colors that accented the color in her smooth cheeks, and the betrothal ring he had given her.

He glanced at the box sitting on the mantel. The ring existed, for he had been want-witted enough to purchase it for Charlene Pye, not realizing she had set her cap for another. No other aspect of Serenity Adams existed, for she was the product of a lonely imagination on nights when his only company had been a bottle of something to sand the edges off his pain.

Now Grandfather wanted to meet her.

Downing the wine in his glass, he sighed. "I see no choice but to go to Cheyney Park and tell Grandfather the truth."

"That is a mistake."

Timothy smiled for the first time in days. "I trust you will tell me that all the way to Cheyney Park."

"You want me to go with you?" Felix shook his head. "I am not the favorite grandson, the beloved heir. Grandfather will waste no time dressing me down."

"For what?"

"For not telling him the truth." He took a deep sip. "He would see that as a gentleman's duty."

"I know." Squaring his shoulders, he said, "I cannot delay this any longer. Wish me good luck, because I shall be leaving at dawn to face his fury."

Felix sighed, then said, "I shall go with you. If I don't and Grandfather learns that I knew of your deception, he will be in a snit at Father for raising such a deceitful son."

"He cannot blame my deceit on anyone but me." He dropped back into the chair. "Blast it! It seemed like such a good idea when I first told Grandfather about meeting this charming young woman who was eager for my attentions."

"If you had not been so busy dealing with Grandfather's business interests, you might have time to meet the young ladies who are seeking a husband."

"I shall leave the flirtations to you." Without looking up, he added, "I am departing for Cheyney Park at dawn. If you wish to go with me, be ready to join me then."

Timothy did not move as his cousin walked out of the parlor. He could not fault Felix for finding the whole of this amusing.

Felix Wayne never would have found himself in such an untenable position, for he could tell falsehoods without hesitation. Only to his father was he unerringly honest. Grasping the bottle, Timothy poured himself another serving of wine. He started to drink it, then set the glass down again. What good was losing himself in wine? All he would have in the morning was a headache and the same problems.

He had not intended this ruse to go so far, but his grandfather had been unduly interested in Serenity Adams and Timothy's intentions toward her. No letter arrived from Cheyney Park without a query about Miss Adams. He should have foreseen this. He might have, if he had not been so caught up in the building of the new textile factory in the Midlands.

You should leave business to businessmen. How many times had Felix chided him with that? It might have been easy to agree if he did not enjoy overseeing the day-to-day management of his grandfather's investments. Mayhap he should have been born a merchant's son, instead of an earl's son's son.

Now he had to face the consequences of his web of lies that had been woven into the image of the perfect woman. He could only hope that his grandfather would forgive him. He doubted if he would ever forgive himself.

Felix cursed as the carriage bounced, and his head cracked against the roof. Glowering at Timothy, who sat across from him, he said, "You should rid yourself of that lame-hand in the box."

"You cannot blame Jenkins for this feather-bed lane." He gripped the window's edge as the carriage dropped into a chuck-hole and out again. Water splattered up from the puddles to blend with the falling rain. "This winter's storms have washed it out."

"We shall not reach the Park tonight at this rate."

"True." He was not sure if that was a relief or not. He did not look forward to confessing to his grandfather, but he did look forward to the relief of being honest at last.

"Blasted inconvenient for the earl to have his birthday on Christmas Eve."

Timothy grinned. "I doubt if his mother took your discomfort today into consideration when the time came for him to be born. Most likely she was thinking only of *her* discomfort."

"By Lord Harry!" Felix bellowed when his head bumped against the carriage roof again. "Can't you tell him to watch where he is going?"

He did not bother to answer. Jenkins was an excellent coachman, and he would be finding the best route along this seldom traveled road that led across the moors not far from the old Roman walls at the farthest extent of their erstwhile empire. The rolling hills edged with low copses and gorse had been swallowed by the fog and freezing rain, and Timothy suspected the coachee could not see much past the tip of the lead horse's nose.

Closing his eyes, he decided to try to rest. He had found no sleep last night either. How long could a man go without rest before his own thoughts drove him to insanity? He had been bird-witted to embark on this journey of lies. Mayhap when he was honest with his grandfather, he would not have to suffer any longer from thoughts of a woman who was nothing but an air-dream. He was the brunt of the jest, because, although he had named her Serenity, he had found no serenity in the past week.

"Why are we stopping?"

Timothy opened his eyes at his cousin's grumble. He was not sure if he had fallen asleep or not. Only a moment might have passed or an hour. Either way, his mind was still groggy, and the heavy rain was still falling, and the fog still reigned across the moors.

He sat straighter as the carriage slowed. It bounced when Jenkins came down off the box.

Opening the door, he called, "Jenkins, what is amiss?"

"Lord Cheyney, there are tracks in the mud here that lead off the side of the road. Looks like a carriage went over."

He raised the collar of his cloak and, ignoring Felix's oaths, stepped out into the rain. Not rain, but sleet. It pelted him like dozens of needles, each cutting into his face. He paid it no more mind than he had his cousin's grousing. "Where?"

"This way." Jenkins was not much taller than a young lad, but he had been driving for more than a score of years. Only such keen eyes would have noted in this storm the path through the half-frozen mud.

Timothy muttered a few curses of his own as he saw the wheel tracks widen. The carriage must have been out of control, slid-ing across the roadway. Rushing to the side of the narrow road, he choked back another curse when he saw a wheel shattered against the stone wall.

"Get the lantern," he ordered.

"Aye, my lord." Jenkins's voice shook as he ran back to the carriage.

Peering through the storm, Timothy could see little. The hill dropped steeply away. Something glittered farther down it. He could not tell whether it was part of a carriage or simply water trickling down the hillside.

He took the lantern Jenkins handed him and stepped over the low wall. Sleet coursed into his collar while it weighed his hair low over his eyes, but he thought only of keeping his footing as he went down the steep hill.

"Wait up!"

He turned to see Felix lurching toward him. "No need for you to get wet until I see what's here."

"Too late." He grinned. "Besides, why should you have all the adventure?"

Although he would have preferred to have Jenkins with him, Timothy nodded. "All right. Take care. It's steep and probably as slippery as a pickpocket's fingers in your pocket." He balanced with one hand on the wall. "Jenkins, stay with the carriage, but listen for our call. We may need help if anyone survived."

"Aye, my lord." The coachman glanced uneasily at Felix.

Instead of replying to his man's obvious question, Timothy began to descend the hill. Felix was no good in an emergency, but denying him the chance to come down here would be a waste of breath. If Felix had a case of the vapors, Timothy would be cursed to perdition before he dragged him back up the hill.

He let his feet slide as he reached from tree to tree. The sleet was thickening to snow, which tried to blind him. The lamplight flickered with his uneven steps. When he saw broken branches and small trees that had been cut off a foot above the ground, he tensed. Something unquestionably had come this way. Something large and out of control, tearing up everything in its path.

A hint of a breeze tugged the curtain of sleet and snow aside, and he saw a broken carriage lying against a tree farther down the hill. A horse thrashed weakly against the harness.

"Jenkins!" he shouted.

"What is it?" Felix asked, slipping toward him.

Timothy pointed. While his cousin cursed with rare spirit, he called an order for the coachee to bring a gun down to end the horse's suffering.

Felix did not follow as Timothy edged down toward the carriage. Timothy stretched to open the door. The carriage shifted against the tree holding it above the creek. He cautiously drew the door aside.

"Is anyone in there?" Felix called.

Timothy did not answer for a long moment as he stared at the bodies clustered together in death. A man and a woman, both well dressed. Feathers on the woman's turban fluttered in the air coursing through the carriage, but that was the only motion within the carriage.

"Yes," he said, as he pulled the door closed, "but they are both dead."

"The coachman is over here," Jenkins shouted, pausing partway down the hill. "He is dead, too."

"Take care of the horse." Timothy sighed. He wished there was something else they could do other than report this to the authorities in the next village. They would have to figure out who had owned this carriage and let the family know of the disaster.

He flinched at the sound of the single shot. Its echo was muted by a woman's shriek.

Whirling, he almost lost his footing. That scream had come from the other side of the carriage. Someone must be alive!

Felix shouted something to him, but he did not pause to listen as he continued down the hill, trying to pinpoint where the sound had come from. He called for Jenkins to fire the gun again. As the shot resonated along the hillside, he followed the terrified cry to his right.

He knew he would never have seen this woman if she had not cried out. Her clothes, as befit a servant, were as drab as the leaves along the hillside. Mud further darkened them. A broken bonnet could not restrain her black hair, which camouflaged her. As she turned her head to look at him, her face was deathly pale. Her shadowed eyes were lost beneath the blood coursing along her forehead.

"Thank goodness," she whispered. "You did not leave me here."

He knelt beside her. "Calm yourself, miss. Where do you hurt?"

When she did not reply, he saw she had lost consciousness. He guessed that only the sound of the gun firing had roused her from her pain. He quickly checked her limbs to determine that no bones were broken. Tearing a strip from the hem of her apron, he bound it around her head to slow the bleeding. He wondered how long she had been lying on the hillside waiting for help that might never have come.

He slipped his arms beneath her and lifted her cautiously. Her moan against his neck sent shivers of dread to his toes. If one of her ribs was broken, he could be hurting her worse. He could not leave her here. Even if they were able to find a doctor in the next village, she might die before they returned.

Her head lolled against his chest. Jenkins scampered across the hillside and down to him. The coachman folded the young woman's arm over her breasts, which rose and fell so slowly. Bending, he picked up her ruined bonnet and one slipper.

"Do you need some help, my lord?" he asked. He tucked the bonnet and slipper under his arm as he gripped the gun with his other hand.

"I think I can manage."

Timothy was less sure of his assertion on every step up the precipitous hill. The woman was slender, but even her slight weight was a burden when he had to fight for each foothold. More than once, Jenkins's hand in the middle of his back steadied him. He was panting like a hound after a fox when he reached the wall at the top of the hill. Somehow he swung one leg, then the other over the wall and carried the young woman to the carriage.

"Oh, my! Oh, my!" Felix said with a gasp as he wrung his hands.

"Calm yourself," he said, as he had to the young woman, even though he knew it was useless. Felix was always ready to cede himself to panic.

"Is she dead?"

"Not yet." He set her on one cushion and climbed into the carriage. Settling her head on his leg, he motioned for his cousin to get in, too.

"What are we going to do with her?"

Timothy exchanged a wry grin with Jenkins. "We are going to the next village to see if we can get some help for her. If we hurry, she may live long enough to get there."

"But, Timothy—"

The young woman shuddered as she drew in a breath, and he retorted, "If we stay here until all your questions are answered, we may be burying her along with the others."

TWO

$\mathcal{P}$ain laced every breath she took. She tried to breathe shallowly, but it made no difference. The pain began on her right side and leaped across to her left with each motion. When she tried to hold her breath, hoping it would ease the anguish, the very pulse of her heart augmented it.

"Shouldn't she be waking up soon?"

She tried to put a face with that petulant voice. For a moment a wisp of memory taunted her; then it vanished into a cacophony of agony. Just thinking hurt.

"Have patience, sir," a woman replied with a comfortingly familiar north country accent.

Did she know that woman? No, she was sure she had never heard the raspy voice before.

Something cool brushed her cheeks. She almost smiled at the brief respite from the pain, but winced as even that slight motion exacerbated the torment.

"She moved! I saw her move!" The man's voice resounded through her aching head.

"Hush, sir. 'Tis best if she wakes slowly."

"At this rate, Timothy will return before she regains her senses."

"If His Lordship is here or not will make no difference in her waking."

She liked that woman's voice. It was matter-of-fact, not borderline hysterical like the man's.

The coolness vanished, and she wanted to ask for it to come back. No words reached her lips. Hearing footsteps fade, she wondered if she had been left alone. How could they leave her alone when she was so helpless? Did they have not a lick of sense between the two of them? Or were there more than two of them with her here in . . . Where was she?

The battering of questions ached worse than her pain and forced her eyes open. She stared up at broad beams crisscrossing a slanted ceiling. Not a hint of whitewash had ever stained them, although a sliver of water edged along one before dripping on the floor. It must still be raining.

Yes, it had been raining before when . . . She frowned. Another moan rushed through her, bursting out of her lips like a peal of thunder.

"Are you awake?"

She wished it had been the woman's voice, but she turned her head to see a man leaning over her. His soggy brown hair clung closely to his scalp and curved along his gaunt face. The intensity in his dark brown eyes threatened to pierce her, and she closed her eyes again. She should scream out her dismay at seeing a stranger leaning over her while she was so vulnerable in this bed, but she did not have the strength.

"I know you are awake," he said.

He *was* petulant. He could have the decency to lower his voice to a whisper that would not careen through her head.

Slowly opening her eyes again, she murmured, "Barely."

"How do you fare, miss . . . ?"

She opened her mouth to answer, then closed it. She knew how she fared. Poorly. What she did not know was the name she should give him.

"Miss . . . ?"

Closing her eyes, she took a careful breath. "I am sorry. I cannot seem to recall my name."

"Is that so?" In a mutter, he added something else, but she could not understand what he said.

She looked across the bed at him. He now had his back to her. Sagging into the pillows, she forgot him as she was overwhelmed with pain again. It dragged her down into the darkness once more.

Not a silent darkness, but one filled with screams and the sounds of a horrible crash. Wood splintering and horses screeching in terror. No escape, nothing but death and pain and more darkness.

"Hush, child," murmured a voice that drew her out of the morass of horror. "'Tis all right. You are safe now."

She gazed up at a woman who was nearly as round as she was tall. A smile stretched the woman's apple red cheeks beneath her gray hair.

"I am the innkeeper's wife, Mrs. Bridges," she said, wringing out a cloth.

She sighed with delight when the cloth brushed her cheeks. Her relief vanished as she heard the irritating man's voice from the other side of the room.

"I need to speak with her alone, Mrs. Bridges."

"But, Mr. Wayne—"

"Alone."

The innkeeper's wife's cheerful expression became a scowl, but she turned away from the bed. The door closed softly in her wake.

"Do you think you can stay awake more than a minute this time?" asked Mr. Wayne as he came to stand by the bed.

"I don't know."

"Then I shall explain this to you quickly. Tell me your name."

"I told you. I don't remember it." She winced, but pushed herself up to sit against the pile of pillows. Looking past him, she saw that the rest of the room was as spare as the ceiling. Plain boards ran along the walls, and the only other piece of furniture than this narrow bed was a washstand by the door. No window broke the wall, but she could hear the sound of something hitting the roof. Something icy. It had been raining when . . . She was not sure when, but she knew it had been raining.

"What do you remember of the accident?"

"I am not sure." Were the nightmare images and sounds memories or just something dredged from her pain?

"Do you remember the names of the people you were traveling with?"

"No." She dampened her lips. "Are they hurt?"

He shook his head. "Not exactly. They are dead."

She pressed her hand to her bodice. Realizing she wore only a nightgown, she pulled the blanket up to her chin. She saw a pile of soaked clothing on the floor. When she looked up at Mr. Wayne, his smile was cold.

"Mrs. Bridges put you to bed here." He sat on its edge. "Listen closely to what I have to say, because I must say it before Timothy returns."

"Timothy? Who is he? Another passenger?"

"Just listen." He smiled as he leaned toward her. "Just listen, and I can guarantee that you will be glad you did."

Timothy swung down off the borrowed horse in front of the Old Vixen Inn. He handed the reins to a stable lad who looked as drenched as he was. For the past two hours he and Jenkins had been helping the local constable and vicar deal with bringing the dead to the village. His pockets were lighter by the cost of three burials. Even though they would be temporary, for their families would want to claim the bodies once the young woman could tell them the names of the dead coachee and the man and woman in the carriage, the corpses could not be left out in the storm.

Nothing in the carriage had given them a clue to the passengers' identities. When he had seen all the footprints in the frozen mud around the carriage, he had guessed thieves had helped themselves to anything of value in it before he was able to return.

"Thank you, my lord, for your assistance," the pudgy vicar said from within his closed carriage. His smile warned that he did not intend to step out into the snow piling up in the yard in front of the inn.

"I wish it had not been necessary."

"The young woman—"

"I left her in Mrs. Bridges's care."

He nodded, both of his chins bouncing together. "Please let her know that I would be glad to speak with her if she wishes."

"And the constable is sure to want to speak with her."

The vicar shrugged. "I doubt if she can tell him anything other than the names of her companions. Then he can contact their families and deal with transferring the bodies. From what we saw on the road, it is clear that your coachman was right. The man in the box on that carriage lost control in the storm. A terrible calamity, but nothing of interest to the law."

Timothy was about to ask another question, but the wind rose, firing snow at him as if from a cannon. The vicar ordered his carriage to hurry him home across the narrow green.

Stepping onto the wide porch, Timothy shook clinging snow and ice from his cape. This storm was not a good omen for his journey to bare his soul to his grandfather.

"Don't be a widgeon," he grumbled to himself as he ducked his head to enter the inn. Superstition had no place in his thoughts, which must be clear when he spoke with Grandfather. Tonight he would enjoy the best this inn had to offer. Even if it was not much, a trencher of beef and some stout would ease the cold left by the storm and the tragedy on the hillside.

Mrs. Bridges hurried to him and held out her hands for his cape. He undid it and shook it again before handing it to her.

"How does she fare?" he asked.

"She is awake."

"Is she?" His smile threatened to crack his taut face. "What has she said?"

Mrs. Bridges frowned. "It was very strange. Mr. Wayne shooed me out of the room before she could say more than a pair of words."

"Why?"

"I don't know." She stepped aside as a lad held out a tankard of beer. "I went to check on her a few minutes ago, and the door was barred."

Timothy glanced at the stairs. "That is odd."

"I thought so." She rubbed her hands together. "Do you know the lass, my lord?"

"No."

"Does Mr. Wayne?"

"I doubt it. He seldom ventures far from London." He took the tankard. Tilting it back, he let the warmth of the beer counteract the hours in the snow and wind. "Why do you think he knows her?"

"No reason. Just the way they were looking at each other."

Timothy cursed and shoved the tankard back into the lad's hands, spilling beer over both of them. Felix had been lamenting for the past week that his latest mistress was boring him. Not wanting to believe that his cousin would take advantage of a lass in such a perilous state, he reached for the rough railing on the stairs.

"They were not looking at each other in *that* way, my lord," Mrs. Bridges hurried to say, warning him that his reaction had been too obvious.

"Then how?"

"Don't know how to explain it exactly."

"Try." *Blast it!* He did not want to stand here playing a guessing game with the innkeeper's wife after he had spent too much time outside on this frosty afternoon.

"As I said, just as if they thought they might know each other."

"Thank you, Mrs. Bridges," he said, as he climbed the stairs.

As dusk drew him up, he wished he had brought the beer with him. The one sip had not been enough to rid him of the chill. His toes were awash in his boots. Once he checked on the young woman and discovered what had unsettled Mrs. Bridges so, he would send his boots to be dried and polished, so they would be ready in the morning when they left. He did not want to delay here any longer than necessary. The sooner he reached Cheyney Park and told his grandfather what he must, the better it would be.

He hoped.

The upper floor was so silent, he could hear the ice pelting overhead. The snow must have warmed to sleet again. It was a good thing he had made arrangements with Mrs. Bridges to spend the night here. Traveling would be even more treacherous as night closed in around them.

The second door on the left was where he had carried the young woman. He knocked on it, but got no reply. Opening it, he saw it was empty. Mayhap it had been the third door. He had been in such a hurry to leave her here and go to the authorities that he had not paid that much attention.

He rapped on that door.

"Who's there?"

"Felix," he said, resisting the temptation to shout, "'tis Timothy." What silly thing was Felix about now? He lifted the latch, but the door would not budge. This was absurd. "Open up."

The door opened only far enough so Felix could peer out. "Are you alone?"

"Of course. I do not need someone to come up here with me because I am afraid of the dark."

"The constable?"

"He and the vicar are back in their comfortable houses. I would like to be equally comfortable with dinner in front of me, but first I would like to speak with the young woman." He put his hand on the door and shoved it and his cousin back slowly. "I understand she is awake."

Felix jerked the door back so suddenly that the wood burned Timothy's hand. "See for yourself."

He took a single step into the room, then paused as he stared at the young woman sitting among the pillows on the bed. Her hair had dried into a cascade of ebony curls around her shoulders. The bandage across her forehead had more color than her wan face, so her lips appeared a vibrant wine red. With the blanket pulled up to her chin, he could not see the rest of her, but he had held her close enough to recall the lithe curves that were hinted at beneath the blanket.

He noticed all that in a single heartbeat. Then he was caught by her wondrous eyes. Not quite blue, not quite gray, they glistened like polished steel in the glow of the single lamp. Even in his imagination, these silver-blue eyes had not been so lustrous.

Felix chuckled, but Timothy could not pull his gaze from the woman on the bed. Those eyes had depths only a fool or a brave man would dare to explore.

"It seems," Felix said with another laugh, "that no introduction is necessary, but, Timothy Crawford, Lord Cheyney, allow me to present to you your fiancée, Serenity Adams."

THREE

*T*hat man was Timothy Crawford? She must have misunderstood. How could *this* be Lord Cheyney? Why would such a handsome man be in such need of a fiancée that he had to hire a stranger to play that role?

Even in the dim light, his hair glowed as gold as an angel's wings. His firmly drawn face was as appealing as the devil's own, and the excellent cut of his clothes could not disguise muscles that appeared to come from long hours of hard work—mayhap outdoors, for his face had a healthy bronze that did not seem to match the life of a London gentleman. A viscount who worked like a laborer? None of this made the least bit of sense.

The man in the doorway continued to stare at her. Why did he look so shocked at Mr. Wayne's pompous announcement? Mayhap Lord Cheyney had not guessed that she would agree to this want-witted scheme.

She would not have, if Mr. Wayne had not brought to her a water-stained letter that had been in the apron of her skirt. It addressed her only as "Dear Sister," but it spoke of how her younger sister and brother were depending on her to send them money to continue their schooling, so they did not have to be sent to the almshouse. The ink had run together, so it had revealed little more than that she had been an abigail to some nameless peer's wife and had planned to send money to her siblings to pay for their next term before the year's end.

Her hope that the letter would give some clue to the identities of the others in the carriage with her had been for naught. If there had been another page with an address on it, that page was not in her apron pocket.

Because of that letter, she had heeded Mr. Wayne's endless prattling about how Lord Cheyney had spun a tale for their mutual grandfather, the Earl of Brookindale. His voice had taken on a wheedling tone that was irritating and seemed to pierce her skull with each word. She could not earn the needed money to send to her brother and sister if she could not recall where she had been in service. When Mr. Wayne had offered her an alternative, she had known she had little choice.

Lord Cheyney rounded on Mr. Wayne. "This young woman has taken quite a knock to her head. What is your excuse for this absurdity?"

"Trying to help you." Mr. Wayne gestured toward her with all the exaggeration of an inept actor. "You need a fiancée, and I have provided you with one. This woman has agreed to pretend to be Serenity Adams for the duration of Grandfather's birthday and Christmas celebrations."

"Why?"

She realized that question was aimed at her. *Bother!* She knew Lord Cheyney was right to ask it. After all, she had asked it as well. Although something churned in disgust in her stomach, she lifted her scratched chin higher as she said, "Because of the five hundred pounds Mr. Wayne has told me you will gladly pay for my help."

"Five hundred pounds?" Lord Cheyney scowled at the shorter man. "Have you completely taken leave of your wits?"

"I am thinking only of how you did not want to upset Grandfather during the celebration of this important birthday." Mr. Wayne's voice was as soothing as if he were speaking with a dim-witted child.

She wondered why Lord Cheyney endured it. When the viscount's brows lowered in a fearful expression, she knew he had heard the condescension as well.

"I do not need you to tell me how best to protect Grandfather from my folly." He came into the room, leaving wet footprints in his wake.

She flinched when he turned to close the door, but he did not slam it. He was unquestionably angry, for each motion was as stiff as if he had been frozen by a winter wind, but he controlled his emotions with an ease that was almost frightening. She could not govern a single one of hers, because each was as new as if she had been born only this morning.

"Are you mad?" Lord Cheyney asked. "I intend to tell Grandfather the truth of my miserable lies."

Mr. Wayne put his hand on the viscount's arm. "But now there is no need. Look at her. She has the appearance of the woman you described to Grandfather."

"Mayhap, but I am going to Cheyney Park to be honest with Grandfather, not to—"

"Ruin his birthday?" Mr. Wayne's voice grew as icy as the sleet striking the low roof. "Timothy, think for a minute, if you will. Why distress Grandfather to the point that he might suffer apoplexy and be bedridden for his birthday celebration? Here is a woman who can prove your lies are the truth."

"But they are not the truth! They are lies."

She stared at the viscount. No one could accuse him of being willing to seek an easy solution to the quandary he found himself in now. If he had those good looks plus this sense of integrity, why had he cluttered up his life with falsehoods? She understood none of this.

Mr. Wayne glanced at her, then back at the viscount. "Timothy, I know that. You know that. *She* knows that. However, Grandfather does not. Why do you want to ruin his birthday gathering simply to alleviate your guilt?"

"And this"—Lord Cheyney gestured toward her—"*this* is supposed to make everything all right? You are mad!"

Mr. Wayne grabbed the viscount's sleeves before he could walk away. "Once Grandfather's celebration is past, you can arrange an argument with Miss Adams that will put an end to your betrothal. You can stage something that will persuade Grandfather that the betrothal was a mistaken thing right from the beginning. That will give you time to find yourself a real fiancée." He laughed tersely. "After all, Timothy, this woman is a lady's maid. Grandfather may decide on his own that she is not the proper one for you to marry."

"But he will not know she is an abigail."

"How many abigails do you know who could act like a lady among the *beau monde*?"

Lord Cheyney arched his brows. "I shall leave the answer to that question to you and your superior experience in knowing the staffs of various ladies' boudoirs."

"So will you look at this as a gift of Providence and take advantage of it?" Mr. Wayne chuckled again. "How many times have you told me that the difference between success and failure is recognizing an opportunity when it comes along?"

Instead of answering, Lord Cheyney looked back at her. She could see distress etched into his face. If he had been on his way to confess his lie to his grandfather, he must be, at heart, an honest man who had been caught up in a single mistake that had compounded to threaten disaster.

Dismay struck her. What if he decided not to accept her assistance in this masquerade? How then would she provide for her sister and brother? She wanted to plead with him to listen to Mr. Wayne, but feared that anything she might say would compel him to decide just the opposite.

Lord Cheyney sighed. "Felix, I should have listened to my instincts weeks ago and told Grandfather the truth straightaway."

"Mayhap, but what are you going to do now?"

Taking another deep breath, Lord Cheyney sighed. "You are right. I would be a beef-head to allow this chance to pass me by when revealing the truth before Grandfather's birthday celebration might cast a horrible shadow over everything that is planned." He scowled at her. "I do not like this a bit."

"That is because you are far too honest." Mr. Wayne slapped him companionably on the arm. With a broad smile, he asked, "Aren't you going to greet your beloved Serenity?"

Lord Cheyney crossed the room to stand beside her bed. "What is your name?" he asked.

"Serenity Adams, my lord."

"No, your real name."

She closed her eyes, wishing all of this would go away and be nothing more than a bad dream. "My lord, I do not know my real name."

"As you said yourself, Timothy, she bumped her head quite hard," Mr. Wayne interjected. "Her injuries from the accident seem to have wiped her memory quite clean. She cannot recall even her name."

Instead of firing another question at her as Mr. Wayne had done, Lord Cheyney sighed. "Miss, you would be wise to rest. We will delay our journey to Cheyney Park until the morrow. Mayhap with some sleep, your mind will heal."

"I hope so." She gazed up at him, wanting to thank him for his unexpected compassion and wanting to apologize for this bumblebath that she had made worse by agreeing to Mr. Wayne's offer.

As if he could sense her thoughts—a most discomforting idea, for she could barely sense her own—Lord Cheyney said in the same subdued tone, "Felix, I would speak with this young woman a few minutes alone."

"I can understand that. You should get better acquainted with your betrothed." His laugh faded away, and he quickly lowered his eyes as Lord Cheyney regarded him with a cool stare.

Uncomfortable silence settled on the room as Mr. Wayne took his leave. Lord Cheyney brought the chair closer to the bed.

"May I?" he asked, motioning to it.

"Of course." She had heard Mr. Wayne tell the viscount that she was a lady's maid, but Lord Cheyney was treating her with the courtesy he would show a lady.

He sat and fisted one hand on each knee. "Let me ask you what I should have immediately. How are you feeling?"

"Confused."

"I meant your injuries."

She touched her brow, then winced. "I have plenty of aches and I suspect many bruises, but the cut on my forehead seems to be the worst injury."

"Other than your missing memory."

"Yes."

He sighed and shook his head. "I own to being at a loss as to how to respond. This is the first time I have encountered someone who has suffered such a loss."

"I would offer you advice, but, if I have met such a person myself, I cannot recall it."

He laughed. "Do not think me too bold to say that you are quite amazing, miss, to be able to be amusing when you are suffering from such a dire experience."

"You are not too bold. If I am to pretend to be your fiancée, you should be comfortable treating me with a certain amount of camaraderie."

"Camaraderie?" He chuckled again. "May I say, miss, that you chose a very tepid word to describe the heartfelt love that should exist between two people who are planning to marry?"

"Love? We are supposed to be in love?" Her eyes widened; then she put her hand to her forehead again. Every motion, even one so slight, continued to make the room spin.

"Miss?"

She heard dismay in his voice, but she could not answer. Clutching the coverlet, she was not sure whether to close her eyes or open them. Either way added to the nausea swarming through her. Myriad images filled her head, but she was not sure what was real and was memory and what was only imagination. Shouts and screams filled her head. Pain slashed through her.

A warm cloth settled on her forehead, and she sank more deeply into the pillows, letting the relief the warmth brought ease the speed of the spinning. Her heartbeat slowed, and she was able to breathe without fearing each breath would be her last. Gone were the maddened scenes that might be memories of the carriage accident or just the remnant of a forgotten nightmare.

"Are you all right?" Cool hands took hers between them, cradling them gently.

"I believe so." Her voice was unsteady even to her own ears. Slowly she opened her eyes to see Lord Cheyney on his feet, his hands surrounding hers. His expression of anxiety spoke more loudly than his words. "Forgive me, my lord. I am afraid I overreacted to your comments."

"You had assumed this betrothal was an arranged one with little affection on either side." One side of his mouth tilted up in a tired smile. "That would have been the better part of wisdom, I see now, but, in an effort to soothe my grandfather's dismay that I had not found someone to wed in the wake of—" He released her hand and cleared his throat. "I thought the tale of a true-love match would please him greatly."

"Because you never imagined it would bring you to this contretemps?"

"Mayhap if I had considered the story of this betrothal of the least importance, I would have given it deeper thought." He folded his hands behind his coat, which was still damp from the winter storm. "I do not condone my cousin's methods, miss, but

Felix is right about one thing. Our grandfather is not a young man. It might be better to humor him on this one thing."

"You care deeply for him, don't you?"

"My cousin?"

She shook her head, then wished she had been more cautious. Leaning her head back again into the pillows, she whispered, "I see that you tolerate your cousin. No more."

"You apparently do not see too clearly just now. Felix and I have been tie-mates as well as cousins for all our lives."

"Really?" she asked, looking up at him.

He was not hoaxing her, for puzzlement filled his eyes. Or was this no more than a part of the greater charade that he was drawing her into? She knew nothing of this man or his cousin or his grandfather. She knew nothing of anything but what had transpired in this rough room since she awoke.

Now it was obviously her turn to apologize. In little more than a whisper, she said, "Forgive me, my lord, if I spoke out of turn. I was judging only on what I saw ensue between the two of you during a very short conversation when, it is obvious, you both were not at your best."

"You have a true skill at understatement."

"I am so uncertain of everything, so it is not easy to compare one thing to another." When his eyes narrowed as he looked down at her, she sat straighter, drawing the cloth off her head, and hastened to add, "My lord, we were speaking of your grandfather. I had remarked that I believed you care deeply for him. Is that so?"

Lord Cheyney sat once more on the chair. "You need not make that a question. I do not recall my own parents, for they both died when I was very young. My grandfather raised me at his country estate of Cheyney Park on the North York moors." His mouth tilted into an ironic grin. "Now I have confused you even further, for I can see that you wonder how I could be false with a man I profess to care for so much."

"It is not my place to question your motives, my lord."

His grin became a grimace. "You should call me Timothy."

"And you will call me Serenity?"

"Will you have trouble answering to that?"

She kneaded her fingers against her drawn-up knees. "No more than answering to anything else, for I would not recognize my own name if you were to speak it to me."

"It seems very likely that you will eventually recall your past."

"I hope you are correct. Now I do not even remember either my brother or sister."

Her voice must have sounded even more despairing to his ears than to her own, because he took her hands in his again and said, "As soon as you remember anything, even the most insignificant fact, come to me. I promise you that I will make arrangements to have you sent back to where you truly belong, so you can continue your life as it should have been." He smiled. "And do not fret about your brother and sister. I will make some inquiries as to what school they are attending in London."

"What makes you think my brother and sister are in London?" She was curious what he had seen in the letter that she had missed.

"May I?" He pointed to the folded letter on the bed.

"Of course."

When he reached past her to pick up the slip of paper, the scents of soap and horseflesh surrounded her. She gazed up at him as he lifted the page from the coverlet and scanned it.

Again, she wondered why he had needed to ask a lady's maid with no memories of her past to pretend to be his betrothed. She was certain—as she was of little else—that this handsome man would have had no trouble persuading a lady to help him ease his grandfather's concerns.

Her fingers tightened on the coverlet. Lord Cheyney's father was dead, and his cousin had introduced himself as *Mr.* Wayne. Lord Cheyney must be the earl's heir. Mayhap that reason was why he had not asked a lady of his acquaintance to assist him. A betrothal to the heir of an elderly earl would be the talk of the *ton*. Its dissolution might very well shame the lady involved.

Why did she know these things with such confidence, but could not recall her own name?

"Ah, here it is," the viscount said, tapping the letter. "I was certain I saw it amid all the blotches of ink. It is impossible to guess if this was written by a child or an adult."

"Saw what amid the blotches?"

"The mention of an outing in the Park. I doubt if it could be any park other than Hyde Park. No other city, but London, to my knowledge, has a park like it, and no other park surrounding the city matches the description here, save for Hyde Park." Folding the page, he handed it back to her. "Once I have had my solicitor determine where they are attending school, I will make arrangements for the money to be transferred to pay for their schooling."

"Before this has even begun?"

His eyes became dark slits again. "Why do you think I should be so suspicious of you that I don't trust you to do as you have promised?"

She started to answer, then realized she had none. Even though she had been distressed by something she could not name when she spoke with Mr. Wayne, Lord Cheyney had treated her with respect and kindness. *Judge a man by the company he keeps.* Whose voice was that? A man's voice that reached out of the jumble of her lost memories, but she could not guess who might belong to it.

"You know nothing of me," she said softly.

"Neither do you know anything of yourself or of me." He sighed. "Do you deem yourself trustworthy?"

"Yes."

"You answered that quickly. Have you recalled something?"

She shook her head as she held the precious page, her only connection with what had been, close to her heart. "I would not have reached the position of abigail if I were deemed untrustworthy."

"True. Therefore I shall trust you with the important details of what I have told my grandfather. Serenity Adams is a young woman who looks much like you. She has been well educated and is respected throughout the Polite World for her gracious skills as a hostess as well as her sense of humor. When we met at Almack's, where Miss Adams was sponsored by her uncle, who is retired from the army, we were much taken with each other. Our first outing together was a luncheon on the banks of the Serpentine with friends." He frowned. "Or mayhap it was at the duchess's rout near the end of the Little Season. Blast it! I never thought I would be called upon to recall every absurd detail."

"I doubt if your grandfather recalls every detail either."

His frown cleared. "You can say that only because you have not met my grandfather yet. He may be reaching the seventieth anniversary of his birth, but his mind is more sharply honed than most men half his age. I am sure he recalls every single detail."

"Then how can you expect to betwattle him?"

"I am not sure *we* can. Felix is often wrong, but in this I believe he is right. I owe my grandfather the truth, but not until after his birthday celebration on Christmas Eve." He hesitated, then asked, "So will you be a part of this madness?"

She did not hesitate, because, like him, the ones she loved depended on her. "Yes."

FOUR

*C*heyney Park was everything Serenity had anticipated. Beyond its ancient gate in what once had been a curtain wall of a hilltop fortress, the stone front of the house that spread across the hill had been darkened by years of sitting alone on its lonely moor. The steep road leading up to it offered a view of the undulating hills leading off into the distance, but she saw no other sign of houses. A few trees had found a foothold against the winds and storms off the North Sea.

"It is fearfully isolated here," Lord Cheyney said quietly.

Serenity peeked back over her shoulder to find him looking at her as if she were a puzzle he could solve if he only stared at her long enough. It unsettled her that he had discerned her thoughts again, as he had too often in the past day while they continued his interrupted journey to Cheyney Park, when she could not unravel the tangle of twisted memories herself.

He leaned toward her, and she fought not to cringe away.

After all, if she were to do a good job persuading others that she was his betrothed, she could not recoil each time he came near. Yet it was difficult to act as if this stranger were her fiancée.

"There," he said, pointing past her.

"What? Where?"

His chuckle warmed her ear before slipping along her neck like the sweetest caress. "Look past that copse. There are several cottages in the dale beyond. Mayhap you will be able to see, through the fog, a sliver of smoke rising from one of the chimneys."

"I see it!" She smiled, trying to ignore her own pleasure at his closeness. That was something she must put an end to at once. This was no more than a pantomime. Not for a moment could she allow herself to forget that he was a viscount, the heir to an earl, and she was a lady's maid. "At least, I think I see it. With the fog it is not easy to tell."

"Those cottages form the edge of the small village that clings to the stream that divides this moor nearly in two. If you follow that stream far enough, I understand it empties into the Tyne before going into the North Sea. That may have been the only connection to the rest of the world in olden times. The locals would send their produce down the stream and—"

"Egad," grumbled Felix from the other seat. "Must you turn everything into a school lesson, Timothy? You know that I care for neither history nor business."

"I am only acquainting her with the facts that she should be familiar with," the viscount replied in the taut tone he had used with his cousin all day. "If she is to be believable as my betrothed, it would be assumed that she is familiar with the places that I have visited often in the past."

"If conversations of such boring subjects is your idea of how a woman should be wooed, 'tis no wonder—"

"Felix," he stated, his tone becoming even colder, "we have only a few seconds before we arrive at the house. Let me use the time to my best advantage."

"Talking about that silly village is your idea of using this time to your *best* advantage?" He guffawed.

Serenity was sure her face must be bright red, for it was as hot as the stones in the box at her feet had been when they left the inn this morning. When Lord Cheyney put his hand on her arm, she stiffened, and he drew it back as if the flame on her face had raced all along her.

His voice returned to its pleasant tone as he went on. "In the village, they have mumming for the Christmastide."

"How wonderful!" She could pretend, as he was, that his cousin had not interrupted with his salacious comments. "I have always enjoyed them."

"Always?"

She smiled. "I seem to find it simple to remember things like that. Things that have only the least importance. I can remember that I like sugar in my tea, but not where I last drank it."

"'Tis a beginning."

Felix grumbled, "Always the optimist, are you not, Timothy?" He stretched and peered out the window as the house blocked the view along the moor. "'Tis about time we arrived. I swear, any part of me that was not bruised by your coachee's poor driving since we left London is cramped from sleeping in that hard bed last night."

Lord Cheyney frowned at him before looking back at her. "He is always like this when he is away from Town. Pay him no mind, Serenity."

Her reply was halted when Felix suddenly smiled. He did that each time anyone used this name she had agreed to pretend was hers. He had spent most of breakfast chuckling while Mrs. Bridges served them and asked if Miss Adams would like anything else. If Felix thought to convince his grandfather that this flummery was the truth, then he must learn to hide that farcical grin.

The more she had had a chance to think of this scheme, the more certain she was that it was doomed to failure. She wished she could tell both the men that, but she must hold her tongue. She needed to keep her sister and brother safe and in the school that obviously cost dear, so she must remain a part of this.

When the carriage stopped in front of a door, she was delighted to see that a porte cochere arched over them. The fog was congealing into cold rain. An icy wind was beginning to keen along the house, and it might turn the rain into sleet again.

She shivered while she hoped no other travelers would suffer on a slick road as she and her companions had.

"Cold?" asked Lord Cheyney.

"Not on the outside."

He ignored Felix, who was groping on the floor for something he had lost. As he moved his leg aside to let his cousin search, he asked, "Memories, Serenity?"

"I am not sure, but I know there are some things I would rather not remember."

"Yes, I am sure you are right about that." Again he seemed to understand what she meant without an explanation. He was very insightful. If his grandfather shared that trait, they were lost before they began.

Before the viscount could say more, a boy ran forward to throw the door open. He peeked in, then dipped his head. "Welcome to Cheyney Park, my lord."

"Is that you, Curt?" Lord Cheyney asked as he stepped out.

No, not Lord Cheyney. She must think of him as Timothy.

"Yes, my lord." The boy straightened with a grin.

"You must be twice as tall as you were the last time I was here." He ruffled the lad's hair.

When Timothy turned to hand her out, she asked, "How long has it been since you were last here?"

"About six months." He chuckled. "Long enough for this lad to sprout up."

Smiling, Serenity—she must always think of herself that way, so she would respond to the name without hesitation—started to answer.

Instead, Felix said, "It seems ludicrous to be sitting here in this damp carriage on this damp day when there are fires on the hearths within."

"Pay him no mind," Timothy replied as he took her hand and helped her out. "He shall find fault with the whole of this visit. Cheyney Park has been home to him as well, but he will claim no address but Town now." He gestured toward the house. "The others you will meet here shall be much more cheerful, I suspect."

"Yes, I hope so." Her heart thudded against her chest as he continued to hold her hand. His long fingers were rough from riding or work, but they held hers as gently as if her hand had been made of the most fragile soap bubble.

"Are you all right?" he asked, consternation stealing his smile.

"Yes."

"You sound quite breathless. If you think the walk up the steps will be too much for you—"

"I shall be fine." *As soon as you release my hand*, she wanted to add. Did all men affect her like this? She wished she knew. Certainly Felix Wayne did not, because she tried to avoid any chance that he might get too close. She was not sure why. If they had met before, she could not recall it. And why should he? She was a lady's maid. He was the grandson of an earl.

Remembering Lord—Timothy's comment about his cousin's habits, which suggested he had led a life as licentious as his comments, she wondered if her lady and Felix had been lovers. That would explain why she was uneasy in his company. Yet that made no sense, for surely he would recognize her.

"Then allow me, Serenity." Timothy drew her hand into his arm.

The lad stared at them as Timothy led her up a pair of steps toward the door. She could not chide the boy, for she knew how poorly she and Timothy matched. He wore a dark coat and breeches that were in prime twig. Her gown, which had been of coarse cloth to begin with, bore the scars of the many repairs Mrs. Bridges had done yesterday.

"Pay him no mind," Timothy murmured.

"Can you ascertain my thoughts even when I don't speak them?" she asked as quietly.

"No, I am only guessing, for I know what I would be thinking if our situations were reversed." He smiled as the door opened. "I would be asking myself how I had come to be in such an absurd assembly of circumstances."

"As I am."

"It takes no great skill to perceive what a perceptive woman like you would be thinking. I am glad you are not want-witted,

Serenity, for you shall need every bit of wits you ever possessed from this point forward."

Her reply vanished as sound erupted out toward them. When she stepped into a foyer, it was as crowded as a village green on a fair day. People rushed up and down ladders and called orders in so many voices that no one could possibly comprehend a single one. Aromas of freshly cut pine were so strong it was nearly intoxicating. Despite Felix's words, the foyer was as damp and chilly as the carriage.

Through the commotion, a short man called, "My lord, welcome back to Cheyney Park. As you can see, you have arrived just in time for the hanging of the greenery in the foyer."

Timothy took off his hat and handed it to a footman. "If I had guessed, Branson, I would have waited another day."

"Or gotten here earlier, more likely." The man pushed his way through the crowd, sidestepping a footman carrying an armload of green branches to another man standing on a ladder and lacing them along the lower edge of the gallery that edged two sides of the foyer. He wore an immaculate coat of unblemished black. In spite of the chaos in the foyer, the dark-haired man had a sense of dignity and tranquillity that labeled him as the butler.

Again, she fought back her frustration at being able to recognize that Branson was Cheyney Park's majordomo. If she knew that, why couldn't she remember something as simple as her own name?

"'Tis not like you to miss a moment of the excitement before Christmas," Branson continued.

"You know me too well," Timothy said.

"No one could have mistaken your excitement, my lord, with the approaching holidays when you were a child."

Serenity pushed her disquiet from her head and listened to the jesting exchange with interest. That the butler was comfortable enough to tease Timothy told her much. In the past day, she had come to believe that Timothy Crawford was a man of uncommon concern for others. It had been that solicitude that led him into this mess of creating a fantasy fiancée.

When he turned to take the cloak that he had lent her, she noted how the servants working to hang the greenery turned and stared as the boy had outside. She wanted to put her hands over the hasty stitching that held the rents in her gown closed. Even if she had enough hands, she must not forget that a lady would keep her poise under the most extreme circumstances.

"Branson," Timothy said, glancing at her, "I trust my grandfather has been informed of our arrival."

"Yes, my lord." The butler kept his gaze steady and aimed at Timothy.

"My cousin is lost amidst this hullabaloo. If you chance to see Felix, let him know that Miss Adams and I are on our way to speak with Grandfather."

"Of course." A hint of a smile tugged at the butler's lips. "Do you wish me to look heartily for him or hardly look?"

Timothy chuckled. "Today it must be the former, Branson."

"As you wish, my lord." He turned and gestured to a couple of the lads who were watching the greens being hung along the banister.

Leading her through the press of people, Timothy continued to laugh under his breath. He said, as they gained the first step of the staircase that curved up toward the right, "You may see it as unseemly to jest so with a member of my grandfather's staff, but—"

"You need not explain, my . . . Timothy," she corrected herself hastily when his brows started to lower.

Another laugh came from behind them—Felix Wayne's arrogant laugh. "That has a decidedly possessive ring to it, Miss Adams." His lips drew back in a grimace as he spoke her name. "Mayhap that jealous nature will be the very thing that brings an end to your betrothal."

"'Tis not the time to speak of such things." Timothy's hand over hers tightened like the muscles along his jaw.

Looking from one man to the other, she wondered how Timothy tolerated his cousin's pomposity. There must be some reason, but she could not fathom what it might be. Telling herself not to make this more complicated than it already was, she took a deep breath when they reached the top of the stairs.

"Grandfather is probably in his office enjoying a pipe at this hour," Timothy said.

Serenity nodded, although questions pelted her lips as the icy rain did the Palladian window that was set above the front door. It had been hidden by the porte cochere, but would offer anyone who stood by it an excellent view of the road leading up to the house and the moor beyond the curtain wall. If she had half a lick of sense, she would rush back down these stairs and along that road to . . . Where could she go when she had no idea where she should be?

When they paused before a heavy oak door, she took a steadying breath. The charade was about to begin, and she must not make a single error, although, she realized, she already had. Lost in her musings, she had not taken note of the turns they had taken along the corridor that led away from the stairs. The house had looked convoluted from the outside. She could not imagine how much more twisted and interconnected the passages would be within its walls.

"Come in."

Serenity barely heard the words through the thick door, and they were repeated in an impatient tone as Timothy was opening the door. Her eyes widened as she saw the large room, which did not appear to be an office, but instead a gracious parlor. No desk or bookshelves suggested this was a place where work was done. Rather, settees and chairs were grouped in front of the white marble hearth and near the trio of windows that created a bay. Thick carpets covered the floor, crisscrossing each other in a haphazard pattern that somehow led directly to the center of the room.

A man sat on a chair facing the fireplace. Smoke wafted around his head, sending the scent of sweet tobacco toward them. She took a deep breath of it and was amazed at the sense of comfort it brought. She must have known someone who used this same tobacco. Later, she would ask Timothy what type of tobacco mixture his grandfather used. If it was a rare combination of tobacco leaves, it might provide a clue to her lost past.

A tug on her arm warned her that she had been standing and staring for too long. She struggled to breathe—in and out, slow and deep—as Timothy led her toward the white-haired man who was regarding them with eyes as earth brown as both his grandsons'. A cane was set next to where his feet were propped up on a stool, but there was no weakness in his motions as he drew the pipe from his lips and set aside the book he must have been reading.

He stared at her until she wanted to step behind Timothy to hide from those uncompromising eyes. Unlike the others in the foyer downstairs, he did not try to hide his curiosity at her unsuitable appearance.

"I had not expected you for another hour," the white-haired man said.

"We rushed to beat this next storm to Cheyney Park." Timothy smiled as he drew her forward another step. "Grandfather, allow me to introduce Miss Serenity Adams. Serenity, my grandfather, Harold Crawford, Earl of Brookindale."

The earl pushed himself to his feet, looking very spry for a man of his advanced years. He smiled. "I have been awaiting this meeting with much anticipation, Miss Adams."

"My lord," she said, dipping into a deep curtsy. She feared she had made a horrible mistake when the room spun like a child's toy.

A hand captured her elbow, keeping her from collapsing to the floor. When an arm went around her waist, she fought to keep from screaming. A jagged breath cut through her, and she doubted if she could have cried out. The ache threw itself down her left leg even as it exploded in her head.

She leaned her face against a firm chest. Timothy's, she knew, but was shocked when a memory told her that she had rested her cheek against him before. He must have carried her from the wrecked carriage to his. If he had not chanced to stop . . . She grasped the front of his waistcoat before the whirl of the room made her ill. She must not think about what would have happened if he had not found her.

Timothy cursed under his breath when Serenity's legs sagged against him. He had told her to have her wits ready for this introduction, but apparently he had forgotten to have his own prepared as well. Putting his arm beneath her knees, he scooped her easily into his arms.

Grandfather grasped his cane and took a pair of steps toward him. "I trust she does not swoon at every introduction."

"No, sir." He stared down at Serenity's face, which was bleached with pain. In the shadow of the shallow brim of the bonnet he had obtained for her from Mrs. Bridges, he could see the angry color of the cut along her forehead. "Serenity was the victim of a carriage accident."

His grandfather's face became as ashen as Serenity's. "How did that happen? Jenkins controls a carriage with rare skill."

"Not Jenkins, Grandfather. Serenity's carriage went off the road and—"

"She was not traveling from London with you?"

Again Timothy wanted to spout his prayers backward, but he must act as calm as his supposed fiancée's name. He hated having to compound his lies with more out-and-outers. Yet this had gone too far to turn back now. "We had planned to meet just north of York. We chanced to find her carriage overturned off a slippery section of the road."

"Her companions?"

"Dead." Felix stepped forward, surprising Timothy, because his cousin usually did not wait this long to become a part of any conversation between Timothy and their mutual grandfather. "That she is alive is a miracle."

Grandfather scowled. "This young woman was in a carriage accident, and the two of you brought her here to jaw over formalities that could have waited until she was feeling better? Timothy, I expected better of you."

Felix grumbled, and Timothy did not have to look at his cousin to know he was scowling. This was one thing that Timothy did find vexing about his cousin. If Grandfather complimented—or even chided—Timothy, Felix acted affronted that he was not included. Timothy could not guess why his cousin wanted to be dressed down for being a widgeon.

"Serenity has been eager to put the anxiety of her first meeting with you behind her with all due speed," he said. That, at least, was the truth. Her fingers had dug into his arm more on every riser.

When she shifted in his arms and moaned softly, Grandfather said, "See to her comfort, Timothy, and then return here. I have several matters I wish to discuss with you alone."

"Yes, Grandfather." As he turned toward the door, he caught a glimpse of Felix's face in the reflection of a mirror set by the windows. His cousin was glowering.

He was tempted to tell Felix that his cousin was welcome to stay here and speak with Grandfather alone. His own conversation with Grandfather was one that Timothy did not anticipate with pleasure.

FIVE

Serenity opened her eyes, but the world was still in motion. She looked up at the ceiling. It was not the painted one of the earl's parlor. What . . .?

"Take care!" came a warning that echoed close to her ear.

She gasped when she realized she was being carried along a passage. Carried by Timothy! "Sweet heavens! What happened?"

"You nearly toppled on your pert nose in front of my grandfather." He chuckled. "If I had not caught you, you would have made an indelible first impression in the middle of his rug. How are you feeling?"

"Good enough to walk on my own, I daresay."

"Do you daresay?" His smile grew tight. "I daresay I would rather not test that on the runner in this hall." When she opened her mouth to reply, he cut her off with, "Here we are."

She hunched and drew in her feet as he paused by a door, but he bumped neither her head nor her toes when he pushed it open. When he kicked it closed behind them, she asked, "Do you think that was wise?"

"What?"

"Closing the door. We are supposed to be only betrothed, Timothy, not wed."

"I shall open the door again once you are settled comfortably. With your skittishness, you must have safeguarded your lady's virtue well." Instantly he added, "Forgive me, Serenity, for my thoughtless words. I should not remind you of your loss."

"'Tis no loss, for I cannot recall anything about the lady I served."

"That may be to your benefit now as you make yourself at home in your rooms."

Serenity looked around the chamber that was beautifully decorated, completely unlike the plain room at the inn. Windows arched toward the distant ceiling. They were swathed in navy velvet that brushed the carpet, which was only a shade lighter. White furniture seemed to be floating on that sea of blue. Chairs were scattered about next to small tables where books were stacked. A dressing table was set beside a trio of windows where the drapes had been pulled back to allow in the faint sun's glow through the swirling clumps of snow.

When he carried her across the Persian rug set atop the carpet by the door, she bit her lip to silence her dismay. She might be a lady's maid, but even a lady's maid knew that a gentleman should not be carrying her toward a bed in a deserted bedchamber.

"Timothy, I can manage to get to a chair on my own now."

"Your words sound more certain of that than your voice. You still have a gray tint to your face. Allow me to do the right thing." He laughed without mirth. "For once through this whole debacle."

His self-deprecation dismayed her. She had most likely made the situation worse. How could she make it better? He would not want her sympathy, because that would exacerbate his remorse at lying to his grandfather.

Forcing a smile, she asked, "You like playing the hero, don't you?"

"It seems I have no choice." He set her on the pale coverlet atop the oak tester bed. "You keep offering me the opportunity by threatening to swoon at the most inopportune moments."

She let the pillows enfold her. "I will try to recall that I should threaten to swoon only at the most opportune moments."

With a chuckle, he leaned one hand against the headboard. "How did you curb that tongue of yours when you were in service?"

"I don't know."

Timothy swallowed his curse as the desolate expression stole the light from Serenity's eyes. *Blast!* He could not let her light-hearted jests tease him into hurting her by constantly reminding her how much had been taken from her in that accident. Not only her employers, who must have thought highly of her to have her riding in the coach with them, but she had lost her very self.

"I am sorry," he said softly. "Again. I fear, no matter how I try to watch my words, I will continue to say the mistaken thing."

"You need not be sorry." She put her hand over his on the bed. "I appreciate all your kindnesses, Timothy. You have been a tip-top gentleman about the whole of this. I know you hate lying to your grandfather as you are."

"It shows that much?"

She nodded.

"If he is as perceptive as you, this scheme shall be for naught."

Pushing herself up, she said, "I promised to help you, and I shall."

He knew he should answer, but he could not find a single word as he looked down into those silvery eyes he had never guessed he would see beyond his fantasies. His gaze slid along her slender nose to the warm curve of her mouth. It was a mouth that invited his kiss. And why not? This was the very woman he had created from his imagination. How many nights had he and Felix spent sitting in his book-room and making up details about Serenity Adams and the outings Timothy had enjoyed with her on their way to a betrothal? Egad, how would he recall the lot? Mayhap Grandfather had kept the letters. If so, he would have Branson obtain them for him.

"Let me help," he said when she fumbled with the ribbons on her bonnet.

"Thank you."

He bent to look at the tight knot. Prying it apart, he said, "You have made a complete jumble of this."

Her laugh stroked the side of his face with its warmth. As he drew aside the ribbons, she reached to lift off her bonnet. He halted her when his fingers edged slowly up her cheeks to lift it away. Her eyes widened at his presumptuous touch, and her hands settled on his. He smiled when she did not push him away. As the bonnet fell away to roll down the pillows to the coverlet, he let his fingers sift up through her sable hair. Her lips parted in the unspoken offer that had haunted his dreams, an offer that sent craving through him.

A throat cleared behind him. He looked over his shoulder to see a middle-aged woman standing in the door of what he knew was the dressing room. He was torn between laughing and cursing at his grandfather's wisdom. Mrs. Scott would be the best watchdog for any young woman in this house, for she had much experience keeping the maids and the footmen from entanglements that would create a to-do in Cheyney Park.

As he reached past Serenity to pick up her bonnet, he knew Mrs. Scott had not arrived a moment too soon. He might be out of his head to have considered kissing Serenity, but it was the only thought in his head now.

"Lord Cheyney," Mrs. Scott said in her no-nonsense voice.

"Mrs. Scott." He nodded toward her, the temptation to laugh growing stronger. She could not rid herself of the habit of treating him as if he still were a child. If she could be privy to the thoughts in his head right now, she would know there was nothing childish left about him.

She bustled into the room and over to the bed. She did not quite elbow him aside, but he suspected she would have if he had not stepped back.

"You must be Serenity Adams," Mrs. Scott said as she took the bonnet from him.

Serenity glanced from Timothy's twitching lips to the pursed ones of this imposing woman. Although Mrs. Scott was shorter than Timothy and wore a dress the same color as her gray hair, she seemed to take control of the chamber with her calm demeanor.

"Yes, ma'am," she replied. No one had to tell Serenity that Mrs. Scott was the housekeeper, for she had the air of a woman firmly in charge.

"Lord Brookindale asked me to see if you had everything you need, Miss Adams." She scowled at Timothy. "He said nothing about your needs, my lord."

Serenity was sure her cheeks were as fiery red as a wintry sunset. When Timothy laughed, she wondered if her mind had been injured in the carriage accident as well as her forehead. No one here reacted as she expected them to.

"I see," Timothy said, "you remain as outspoken as ever, Mrs. Scott."

"One learns to be outspoken here if one wants to be heard over the hubbub." The housekeeper lowered her voice to a conspiratorial whisper. "They both are due to arrive within a week."

"Both?"

"Your aunt from the Continent and that woman your cousin Felix seems to have developed some affection for." Her nose wrinkled as if the house were about to be invaded by some sort of plague.

Timothy's smile wavered as he glanced at Serenity. "You might as well know the truth right from the onset. Mrs. Scott speaks of my aunt Ilse, who married into the household of some minor Prussian state that I am sure you have never heard of. None of us had until she announced her plans to marry Prince Rupert."

"And the other?" Serenity asked. She wanted to know as much as she could about this household and its residents and guests so she did not ruin his plan.

"The other is Melanda Hayes, who is, without question, one of the most vexing people in England." He winked at Mrs. Scott. "Or mayhap in the whole world."

"You have traveled farther than I have, my lord," she said in the same precise tone. "I will have to leave that judgment to you while you leave Miss Adams to me. The earl wants her to rest after her ordeal."

"So rest she shall." Timothy chuckled. "How are you, Mrs. Scott? You look well."

"Other than the knee . . ." She set the bonnet on the dressing table and smiled. "Life would not be interesting if it were perfect."

"And the plans are going well?"

Mrs. Scott glanced at the bed.

"I have taken Miss Adams into my confidence about many of the details of the plans for Grandfather's party." Timothy's smile wavered again, and Serenity guessed he would tell her the whole of it as soon as he could, so he did not have to be false with the housekeeper. "You can speak plainly in front of her about any of it."

"But not now!" She wagged a finger at him. "My lord, the earl wishes Miss Adams to rest *now*."

"I understand." He brushed Serenity's face with the back of his fingertips. "Rest well, sweetheart."

Her heart thudded against her chest. Because of his touch? Because of his words? She must have hit her head even harder than she had guessed if she would give credence to either. This was a game only.

"Yes," she whispered, "I shall rest." Mayhap, when she woke, she would have herself back under control, so she would not react so strongly to what was only playacting.

Shutting her eyes, she watched from under her lashes as Timothy turned away from the bed. He walked away only a few steps, motioning for Mrs. Scott to come over to where he stood. Only by straining could she hear their low voices.

"Miss Adams will need to replace her wardrobe that was destroyed in the carriage accident," he said.

A wardrobe! Her eyes popped open. She had not realized how much this deception would cost Timothy. It was only a few weeks until Christmas. To spend all that money on a wardrobe for her that she could not use when she regained her memories and went back into service seemed ludicrous.

"Of course." Mrs. Scott smiled at her. "If you will give me the name and address of your modiste, Miss Adams, I shall have a message sent for her to come here."

Serenity bit her lower lip. A seamstress? She had no idea of the name of any.

"My dear Serenity," Timothy said so quickly that she doubted if Mrs. Scott had noticed her hesitation, "I recall you telling me that you had admired a bosom-bow's dress and had learned of Madame DuLac's skill with a needle. Mrs. Scott, I shall give you the address. I believe Miss Adams should rest now."

"Those were your grandfather's orders." Mrs. Scott's eyes twinkled. "If you will be so kind to recall *that*, my lord."

"I doubt you would allow me to forget." Timothy grinned again. "I shall leave Miss Adams to your capable care while I retrieve Madame's address."

Serenity let her shoulders relax back into the pillows as he walked out of the room, which seemed so empty without him. *Don't be absurd!* With the fire dancing on the hearth as the wind teased the windows, this was probably the finest room she had ever been in.

Mrs. Scott walked over to the bed and smiled. "May I say that, despite the mishaps you suffered on your way here, you look well?"

"Thank you." Cheyney Park must have the most efficient system of gossip in all of England. Serenity was unsure if anyone had mentioned the carriage accident. How long had she been senseless?

She looked at a gilded clock on the mantel and relaxed again. It must have been for only a few minutes that she had lost consciousness. Wrapping her arms around herself, she thought of how perfect it had been to be cradled in Timothy's strong arms. The beat of his heart beneath her ear had been sweet music, urging her heart to match its rhythm. It had been wondrous.

"We have been looking forward to your visit, Miss Adams." The housekeeper's voice ripped her away from her reverie of forbidden dreams.

"You have?" She hoped Mrs. Scott had not said something else she had missed.

"I don't usually talk out of turn, but the earl is always happy to see his grandson, the viscount, and more so than ever this time when Lord Cheyney has brought you to meet his grandfather."

"I hope I can meet his expectations." That was the most honest thing she had said since she woke in the inn.

"Don't mind the earl's bluster, Miss Adams. He is deeply devoted to those of his family he respects. The others . . ." She shrugged and began to undo Serenity's left shoe. Setting it on the floor, she reached for the other one.

Wanting to ask who the others were, because she was hungry for any information that might help her keep from revealing the truth of this deception, Serenity simply smiled. A lady would not gossip with a servant. Again that was something she knew with a certainty that was inexplicable when so much of her past was gone. Mayhap she had been a prattlebox, and her employer had chastised her with a similar comment. Odd, though, for she did not seem to be a prattlebox.

It did appear that, given the opportunity, Mrs. Scott was. Or mayhap it was nothing more than that she was trying to offer a welcome to the woman she believed would be the next chatelaine of Cheyney Park. As she drew the covers all around Serenity, the housekeeper said, "I shall send Nan to help you, Miss Adams. She is young, but not without experience as an abigail. The earl hired her last year when . . ." She glanced at the clock on the mantel. "Dear me, look at the time. I told Cook I would be up here for only a few minutes. Is there anything else you need just now?"

"Lord Brookindale's prescription for me to rest sounds wisest just now," Serenity replied, trying to keep her smile in place. All she wanted to do was close her eyes and fall asleep. Then she could forget the whole of this. "I want to recover quickly from this accident, so I can watch the house being decorated for the holidays."

"The holidays!" Mrs. Scott rolled her eyes. "I dread them every year. It is busy enough with Christmas and New Year's Day and Twelfth Night, but the earl's birthday makes things even more hectic."

"Especially this year when he reaches the seventieth anniversary of his birth."

"Especially this year when the whole family seems to be descending on Cheyney Park." The housekeeper shook her head and sighed. "If only *they* were not coming, there might be hope of a calm holiday."

"They?"

The housekeeper glanced toward the door and lowered her voice. "Those two, Miss Adams."

A lady would not gossip with a servant. In spite of her curiosity, she said, "I hope that things go better than you expect."

"So do I, but I expect, Miss Adams, that you are going to have a Christmastide unlike any you have ever known."

"What do you mean?"

Mrs. Scott's smile returned. "You shall see."

SIX

$\mathcal{T}$imothy set the two leather-bound books on the desk in his bedchamber. With a wry grin, he opened a drawer and put them inside, out of view. Grandfather would be upset if he discovered Timothy had brought work with him to Cheyney Park. In only one way did Timothy see a resemblance between Grandfather and Felix: both of them believed that work belonged to the working class, not to the *ton*.

"You have no idea of all the fun that you are missing," he mused.

"Did you say something, my lord?"

"Nothing, Henry." He leaned on the desk and watched as Henry unpacked the rest of his bags.

Henry was no longer a young man, but no sign of age slowed him. He still bounced around the room, doing all his tasks with a sense of happiness. He acted as young as a youth, even though his face was lined with wrinkles and his hair was losing its ginger shade to a silver almost as bright as Serenity's eyes.

Blast it! He should not be letting his mind linger on Serenity, but thinking of anything else seemed impossible. She had lauded him for his kindness. She must not guess that there had been two reasons why he had acquiesced to Felix's absurd plan. One had been, he had to own, a kindness, because he could not withdraw the generous offer of money that Felix had suggested as payment for her services. Seeing her dismay when she had thought Timothy would reject the whole scheme, he had understood her desperation when she spoke of her fear for her siblings she could not even recall past the words in that letter.

The other reason had been far less altruistic. Having seen how Serenity resembled the woman he had devised out of his dreams, he wanted to discover what this real woman was like. Would she be tenderhearted? Or coldhearted, as Charlene Pye had been when bidding him to give up his work and become a "real gentleman of the *ton*," as she had said so pointedly? Only then had he understood that Charlene was jealous of any time he was not sitting by her side, plying her with court-promises and nothing-sayings.

"You are deep in thought, my lord," Henry said as he closed the door to the armoire, where he had been placing the last of Timothy's clothes. "Is there a way I can be of assistance?"

"Not unless you wish to take my place when I explain to Grandfather why I have been keeping him waiting."

"He would expect you to be certain that Miss Adams is well taken care of, no matter how much time that requires him to wait."

Timothy smiled. "Have you always been so devious, Henry?"

"I am afraid so, my lord."

"I shall have to remember that." He clapped his valet on the shoulder. "That might come in handy someday."

That his grandfather was waiting with patience did not surprise Timothy. Lord Brookindale had told him often that all things came to a man who knew how to wait and that it was a fool who chased after things before their time had arrived.

Timothy let a smile tip his lips when a servant stepped forward with a tray that held a single glass of brandy. Taking it with a nod, he sat in a chair facing his grandfather, who was sipping his own glass with appreciation.

"I trust Miss Adams is doing better," Grandfather said quietly.

"I would express her apologies."

"For what?" Grandfather's eyes sparked with dark fire. "For betrothing herself to a beef-head who thinks of greeting his grandfather instead of tending to his betrothed, who has endured an upset carriage?"

"The point is taken, Grandfather."

"I thought it would be."

"And I have apologized to Serenity."

His grandfather leaned back in his chair and held up his brandy, so it caught the flicker of the firelight. "She is everything you wrote that she was."

"You can determine that after exchanging so few words with her?" Wanting to ask what his grandfather had perceived so swiftly, he could not. The wrong word would allow the insightful earl to see through their scheme, which had as little substance as a spider's web.

"Is something amiss, Timothy?"

His fingers clenched on his glass. "Why do you ask?"

"You are as evasive as a thief surrounded by the watch. A simple comment brings forth a sharp question from you."

"I am curious how you intuited so much about Serenity during such a brief conversation."

Grandfather smiled. "I did not. I saw she is as lovely as you described, so I assumed you have not exaggerated any of her other virtues. During the past seven decades, I have discovered that if there is one thing a man embellishes about the lady he loves, it is her appearance."

"Again a point well taken." Letting his shoulders ease from their rigid stance, he smiled.

His smile stayed in place as his grandfather turned the conversation to the jumble in the foyer, where Branson was overseeing the hanging of the greens. By the time he had finished his brandy, his grandfather's eyes were growing heavy with the passage of the afternoon. Timothy bade his grandfather to have a pleasant nap and took his leave.

Timothy whistled a light tune under his breath as he strode along the hall. He jumped aside as a warning was shouted. Holly cascaded around him. Waving aside a lass's hurried apologies, he picked up the holly and handed it back to her. She dipped in a curtsy and gave him a smile that suggested she would be grateful for anything he wanted to offer her.

Blast it! He had enough trouble with the single woman in his life. He did not need to complicate things more by a flirtation with a serving lass.

When his name was called, he wondered how a day could go from one disaster to the next with such speed. He waved to his cousin, who was coming in the opposite direction along the hall. From the expression on Felix's face, Timothy guessed his cousin had been waiting, but with far less patience than Grandfather had shown.

"I thought you would be done long ago," Felix complained as he opened the door to a small parlor. Although a fire was burning on the hearth, the room had the odor of one that had been closed for too long.

Timothy frowned. He had not thought of how empty this house must seem to Grandfather, who had been accustomed to his large family, but which had dwindled to so few. Timothy and Felix and Felix's father were seldom here, so that left the staff and Grandfather and mayhap Cousin Theodora and her mother, although he had seen no sign of either of them.

Felix dropped into a leather chair and smiled. "Serenity's first meeting with Grandfather went well." He rubbed his hands together. "Did you arrange with her to feign vapors like that to garner Grandfather's compassion?"

"Nothing was arranged or feigned."

"Is she that badly hurt? Having her die now would truly ruin Grandfather's birthday party."

Timothy grimaced. "I am sure Serenity shall be gratified to hear of your concern for her continued well-being."

"Bah!" Felix waved a dismissive hand toward him. "You understand very well what I mean."

"I do understand very well what you mean, and I trust you shall understand what I mean when I ask you to excuse me. I have matters to deal with."

"Work?"

"You need not make it sound like an oath."

"You are on holiday, Timothy. That accursed factory will run without you hovering over it like a worried mother."

"Have a pleasant afternoon." He left his cousin to fume alone. Arguing over this was a waste of time, because, if Charlene Pye could not change his mind, Felix should know that he could not.

He continued along the hallway, noticing again how empty the house seemed. Was it just the house, or was it he who was empty?

"It will have to do." Mrs. Scott clucked her tongue in dismay as she moved to view Serenity from another angle. "Nan, there is nothing else?"

The maid shook her head. "That is the last of the lot that Mrs. Danton left behind."

Serenity looked down at the light blue gown and brushed her fingers along the sprigged linen, which was highlighted with white blossoms. "It is lovely."

"But it does not fit you!" moaned Mrs. Scott. "It is too full at the waist, and Nan left the hooks undone at the top, for they will not close at the bodice. You cannot go out of this room half-dressed."

"Do you have a shawl amid all those things?" Serenity asked, turning to look at the bed that was nearly lost beneath the clothing that Nan had brought to the room. The abigail was not much taller than a child, and when she carried all those dresses that apparently belonged to one of Timothy's cousins, she looked like a stack of clothing with legs.

Nan rushed to the bed, reached in, and plucked out a white lace shawl. Smiling, she brought it to Serenity.

"If," Serenity said, "you can latch the top two hooks, I think this will cover the rest of them."

Mrs. Scott's eyes threatened to bounce right from her skull. "Miss Adams, you still would be half-dressed."

"But no one shall be the wiser." When the housekeeper opened her mouth to argue, Serenity added, "Would you rather that I wore my mended dress to dinner with the earl?"

Taking a deep breath, Mrs. Scott released it slowly. "No, you cannot wear rags to dinner with Lord Brookindale. Very well, but keep the shawl about you at all times."

"I promise to you that I shall. I don't want to do anything to shame Timothy."

Mrs. Scott's smile returned, but she did not answer as a knock sounded on the door to the hall. Motioning Nan to open it, she settled the shawl over Serenity's shoulders.

Serenity smoothed it around her just as she heard Timothy ask, "Will you inquire if Miss Adams is ready for an escort down to dinner?"

Glancing into the glass once more and making sure that her hair covered the small bandage Mrs. Scott had placed on her forehead, Serenity found herself instead admiring Timothy's reflection. His black coat was the perfect contrast to his tawny hair. His buckskin breeches were topped with a crimson-striped waistcoat. The hint of gold must be his watch chain.

She would have liked to stand there and drink in the sight of him, but she was aware of Mrs. Scott and Nan—*and Timothy*—watching. She went to the door. "Thank you, Timothy. I hope you will escort me every evening until I know my own way."

"And beyond that," he said with a smile. It broadened as he eyed her from head to foot and then back again. "You look lovely, Serenity."

"I never have looked my best with mud and scratches on my face."

He chuckled and offered his arm. "I shall endeavor to remember that."

Putting her hand on his arm, she let him sweep her out of her room and along the hall. He soon had her laughing as he pointed out portraits of some of his less illustrious ancestors, portraits that had been banished from the more public regions of the house, but could not be put in the attics. He regaled her with the story of a several-times great-uncle who had tried his hand at finding gold in America and had found only icy winters that sent him fleeing back to Cheyney Park.

Voices reached toward them as they came down the stairs, and Timothy grew suddenly somber when he asked, "Are you sure you feel well enough for this?"

"I will reassure your grandfather that *I* insisted on coming down for dinner. If you would like, I can add that you tried to persuade me to remain in bed."

His smile flickered across his lips. "Trust me, Serenity, if I had tried to persuade you to remain in bed, I would not want my grandfather to witness my failure."

Heat flashed along her face. "You are misconstruing my words."

"I know."

She scowled at him. "A fiancée should be granted a certain level of respect that does not include such comments."

"You need not fritter away your ladylike airs on me. Save them for Grandfather."

"Timothy, what is wrong?" she asked, tightening her hold on his arm to keep him from walking away. "Did something happen while I was resting?"

"Yes, my grandfather swallowed the whole of this clanker."

She dampened her lips, then whispered, "If you want to have that brangle now that will put an end to the betrothal, you need only say so."

"And what would you do then? You have not recalled anything of where you have been living, I assume."

"Nothing."

His hand curved along her cheek as he smiled sadly. "It seems we both are captives of our own machinations." His hand dropped away. "Shall we?"

"Yes." She hesitated, then said, "Timothy, I do not mind if you blame any mistakes I make on my uneven memory after the accident."

"I would prefer not to make your misfortune my good fortune."

"We shall need all the good luck we can find."

He put his hand over hers on his arm. "Sweetheart, for once we are in utter agreement."

As before, the endearment sent a warm flush through her. Telling herself not to be ridiculous, for she realized he had spoken thusly because they were within earshot of those within the parlor ahead of them, she could not keep from imagining how wondrous it would be to have a handsome man like Timothy Crawford addressing her like that with complete sincerity.

Serenity had no time to do more than form that thought, because Timothy drew her into the room, which was decorated with oak throughout. Pottery that she recognized as being from the Far East, although she had no idea how she knew that, was scattered over every surface. Blue and white mixed with jade, each fanciful figure capturing and holding the light from the brass chandelier that hung from a medallion in the very center of the ceiling.

"How beautiful!" she said with a gasp. "That female temple lion is exquisitely carved."

Lord Brookindale came forward with a glass of wine, which he offered her. As she took it, he asked, "Do you assume that the sculpture is female because of the filigree of curls in the mane?"

"No," she said, releasing Timothy's arm and squatting to point at the small creature beneath the lion's raised paw. "See the cub there? That means the statue is meant to depict a female. A male usually has an orb beneath his claws."

"You did not tell me, Timothy," the earl said with a smile, "that Miss Adams was so expert in Chinese art."

"Mayhap not, but I *did* mention, I assume, that I have found her to be a constant surprise." He held his hand out to her.

Serenity hoped she had not spoken foolishly. Letting Timothy bring her back to her feet, she started to whisper that question to him. He warned her to silence with the slightest shake of his head.

"I don't know," she murmured when, as his grandfather turned away to go into the elegant dining room she could see through the arched door, Timothy asked her how she had known about the lions. "These tantalizing bits of memory appear, but nothing that will help me know the truth about—" She clamped her lips closed as a familiar laugh sounded from just behind her.

"Good evening, Timothy, Serenity." Felix bowed his head toward each of them.

"Good evening," she replied, but glanced at the woman beside him, her hand possessively gripping his arm. She was tall and slender, with lush curls that were only a shade darker than Timothy's blond hair. Although her nose might be a bit too long for the dictates of society, she was an elegant woman in her gown of flawless white.

"Serenity," Timothy said quietly, "allow me to introduce Miss Melanda Hayes."

Before Serenity could react to the name that had brought a grimace from the housekeeper, Miss Hayes gushed, "So you are the one who captured Timothy's broken heart and put it back together. I doubted it would ever happen, but it seems you did a first-rate job."

"Broken heart?" Serenity asked, glancing at Timothy.

"'Tis nothing," he said, as he drew her arm within his again. "Grandfather does not like to let dinner wait. Shall we indulge him?"

"Of course." She knew this was not the time to ask such questions. If she and Timothy had met in London, certainly she would know all the *on-dits* about the man whom she had promised to wed. She hoped he would explain later. Every word that was spoken had the potential to trip her into revealing the truth.

When Serenity turned to enter the dining room, Melanda cried, "You cannot go in yet!"

"What?" Timothy looked at her as if she were quite mad.

Melanda pointed over Serenity's head. "You cannot tell me that you did not steer your betrothed under the mistletoe apurpose."

Serenity looked up, then at Timothy's shocked face. Lost as they had been in their conversation, he must have taken no more notice than she of the kissing bough hung above their heads in the doorway. Although it was made mostly of the holly that was swagged from one side of the doorway to the other, there was no mistaking the leaves of the mistletoe woven through it.

Felix chuckled. "You know Timothy well, Melanda. He never does anything without a good reason, and it seems as if he has a very good one right now."

"He does, doesn't he?" Serenity returned with a smile she hoped did not look brittle. "However, he will have to content himself with my hand." She held out her fingers to Timothy, "At least until my head has stopped aching." As he took her hand and bowed over it, she laughed. "I fear anything more would set my head to spinning even more than it does now."

Dropping her hand, unkissed, Timothy put his arm around her waist. "Do you need to sit, Serenity? Mayhap you should not have been so insistent about coming down to join us tonight."

She rested her head against his shoulder. "I think I am fine, but you are right. Sitting would be the wisest thing now."

"Nicely done," he murmured as he led her toward the dining room. "And true as well."

"True?" She tilted her head back to see his smile.

"I cannot think of anything that would make *my* head spin more at the moment than stealing a tender kiss from a lovely lady."

She looked hastily away as his teasing words brought forth that dangerous warmth again. Glad for the excuse of being seated in the oak-walled dining room at the table between the earl and Timothy, she let the conversation flow around her as she enjoyed the delicious vegetable soup set in front of her. The food at the inn had been plain, and the meal that the innkeeper had sent with them had been hearty, but the fragrant spices in this were as exotic as the statuary in the other room. Each course was as succulent, and she savored the flavors as Melanda talked about the party that she had attended just before leaving Town and who had been there and who had not.

"You are very quiet this evening, Serenity," said the earl as the dessert plates with the final crumbs of chocolate cake were taken away.

"I am enjoying this excellent repast," she replied. Folding her hands in her lap, she smiled. "You are lucky to have such a skilled cook, my lord."

"*My lord*? I shall hear nothing of the sort from you, young lady. As my grandson's future bride, you should call me Grandfather as he does." He looked past her. "Isn't that right, Timothy?"

"Y-yes."

Serenity glanced at Timothy when she heard the hint of hesitation in his voice. His smile was unchanged, but she noted how his hands clenched just beneath the table. How it must hurt him to be false with his grandfather! Wanting to put her hand over his, she could not as the earl asked her how she was feeling in the wake of the accident.

"Better with each passing hour," she replied.

"It must have been horrible," Felix interjected.

"Yes."

Timothy's arm curved around the back of her chair. "I know you all are curious about the events around the accident, as I am, for I do not want to think of something like that happening to Serenity ever again, but speaking of it is certain to unsettle her. I beg your indulgence in speaking of another subject."

"Of course," the earl said, aiming a glare at his younger grandson. "We *all* will keep that in mind." As he came to his feet, he added, "We shall enjoy so many events in the coming weeks that you shall have no time to let your thoughts linger on what happened, Serenity."

"So Timothy has told me." She was glad when Timothy offered her his hand to help her to her feet. Although she had relished every bite, she had not guessed that the mere task of eating a meal would tire her so much. She wobbled, and he put his arm around her waist again. "Forgive me."

"There is nothing to forgive." Lord Brookindale motioned toward the door. "Timothy, I believe we have kept Serenity too long at our conversation. Will you see that she is settled under Mrs. Scott's care?"

"Thank you," Serenity said.

When the old man smiled, she saw a hint of the dashing rogue he must have been a half century before, when he would have been as handsome as his heir. He folded her hand between his. "Rest well, young lady. I don't want you to miss a moment of the entertainments that these young bucks have planned supposedly for me."

"Felix has been telling me all about the ball on Christmas Eve," Melanda said, clearly distressed at being left out of the conversation, for her lips were pursed in a pout. "It will be the very best of anything planned. Better than the mummeries or anything else."

Chuckling, the earl replied, "I am looking forward to the good food, but I doubt if I shall do anything as strenuous as riding into the village." He looked back at Serenity, who wondered if he guessed what a fierce scowl Melanda was wearing now. "However, from what Timothy tells me of your family's dirty acres, Serenity, I suspect you soon will be in the saddle again. He was relating about your adventures in the hunt with your father's master of the hounds. You should share the tale of that with Melanda and Felix, if Timothy has not told him already."

Serenity did not dare to falter. "My lord—Grandfather, I must own the truth. My memories are a bit unsteady in the wake of the accident. Some parts of my past seem to be gone." She sighed. "So I don't recall ever riding to the hunt."

"Did you know of this, Timothy?" the earl asked, his smile vanishing.

"Yes, Grandfather."

"Have you sent for Mr. Lockins to come and check her to be certain there is no lasting damage?"

Serenity put her hand on the earl's arm. "Unless your doctor can reach into my brain and retrieve my memories, there is little he could do. I assured Timothy of that before we left for Cheyney Park this morning. He would not have allowed me to travel if he had been uncertain of my health."

"And because of that, I must insist that Serenity retire now," Timothy said quietly.

"Of course, of course." The earl waved his hand in their direction. "I wanted to finish that book before I went to bed, so this will give me a chance."

Serenity saw the glance between Felix and Melanda, but could not guess what they were thinking because Timothy led her out of the dining room. He kept his hand on her elbow as he guided her back up the stairs.

"What is wrong?" she asked when they were walking along the upper corridor toward the wing where her bedchamber was located.

"Grandfather is acting oddly," Timothy said.

"I thought he was being most kind."

"He is. Most oddly kind. I understand that he did not give my mother permission to address him as anything but 'my lord' until the day she wed my father. Apparently it was even longer with Felix's mother."

"People grow more mellow and forgiving as they grow older and family becomes so important."

He laughed tersely. "For someone who has lost every bit of her life, you seem to have great insight into the lives of those around you."

"Mayhap it is simply because I am learning everything anew that I am aware of these things. Often one sees things most clearly the first time."

He paused by her door. "As I saw how your shawl covers the back of your gown, which is undone?"

"I did not realize that you had noticed." She was glad the dim light hid any blush that might be coloring her cheeks.

"I doubt if the others took note, but then the others did not assist you from your chair and see how your dress gapped at the back." His arm slipped around her waist and brought her to face him.

She put her hands up, intending only to keep a respectable distance between them, but her rebellious fingers stroked the front of his satin waistcoat. The firm muscles beneath it told her again that he did not lead a sedentary life. Wanting to ask what he did to forge these strong sinews that begged her hands to be even more bold, she found words impossible. She was caught between his sturdy arm and the ebony fires in his gaze.

His finger under her chin tilted her face toward his. "You are so beautiful," he whispered. "Just as I imagined Serenity would be."

"But she is only a fantasy."

"Then that makes you a fantasy come true." He drew her even closer. His fingers brushed the back of her open dress as he bent toward her.

She held her breath, knowing she should push him away. When his lips brushed her cheek, he released her with obvious reluctance. She stared at him, astonished.

"But," he said softly, "you are not a fantasy. You are real, and I am a fool."

"Timothy—"

"Good night, Serenity." He turned on his heel and continued along the passage.

She leaned back against her bedchamber door, not moving until she heard a distant door open and close. So much she had learned about Timothy Crawford tonight—of his devotion to family, of his inability to suffer skimble-skamble comments, of his deep integrity. And she had learned something about herself as well tonight.

She had learned that a kiss on the cheek from him was not enough.

SEVEN

*I*t will do." Madame DuLac tapped her teeth with her needle and shook her head, which was topped with curls of perfect white.

"It is lovely." In the past few days, Serenity had become accustomed to the modiste's ways. Madame must have been born beneath a gloomy cloud, for she saw disaster at every possible turn. She was never happy with anything, even the incredibly beautiful confections she and her team of four seamstresses had created for Serenity since their arrival at Cheyney Park.

"Yes, 'tis the most beautiful thing I have ever seen," Mrs. Scott murmured as Serenity looked over her shoulder into the glass to see the scarlet ribbons running down the back of the white gown. More ribbons were laced through the eyelet along the sleeve cuffs that ended at her elbows and in the ruching at the hem.

The housekeeper had come whenever she could into the room that Madame had taken over as her work area next door to

Serenity's bedchamber. With sunlight reflecting off the snow and pouring through the window, it was perfect for sewing.

"It will do," the modiste announced in the same dreary voice. "Of course, we have time to make it better, because you shall not need this until the evening before Christmas, no?"

"No—I mean, yes." Serenity raised her hands compliantly as the dress was unhooked and lifted over her head. "That is, for the ball to celebrate the earl's birthday."

She was not sure if Madame heard her, because the modiste was talking to her seamstresses in a mix of French and English that Serenity guessed the Yorkshire lasses did not understand completely. However, they seemed to guess what she wanted, because they bent to their work on the three other gowns that still had not been completed.

"Allow me, miss," Nan said, edging forward. The young abigail had been chided once by Madame for being in the way and since had clung to the most distant corner whenever the couturière was in the room. "The pink one, I believe, is your choice for today."

Serenity would have been delighted with any of the rainbow of gowns that were scattered across the settees and chairs of the room. Did any one woman need so many clothes and small clothes? Mrs. Scott had assured her that, with the many events to come during the holidays and the earl's birthday celebration, this wardrobe would be barely enough. It appeared that the betrothed of the earl's heir must not be seen in the same dress twice.

In spite of her thoughts, Serenity could not keep from stroking the soft gauze flowing over her gown. It dropped from the bodice to subdue the already pale pink satin beneath it. With every step, the fabric whispered and fluttered the lazy white lace bow beneath her breasts. The white slippers that Madame had provided were each topped with a small piece of the same lace as her bow.

She thanked Nan, bade Madame a good afternoon, and made her escape. Standing and not daring to breathe while surrounded by dozens of pins seemed the waste of a day, although she was not sure what else she might be doing. She had not seen Timothy, save at meals, for the past two days. What he was doing to keep busy was something he had not mentioned.

Mayhap he was away from Cheyney Park on calls. That made no sense, for he would take his betrothed with him on such visits.

Unless he is calling on someone who would not welcome his fiancée.

Serenity sped along the corridor, but could not evade that thought. Had she lost her good sense as well as her memories? The thought that he might be calling upon a woman should not trouble her.

Pausing by a large window seat, she sat on it and gazed out over the moors. Her smile returned as she admired the untamed beauty. She was being witless. Timothy was so determined to prevent his grandfather from being disturbed by his falsehoods that he had agreed to this arrangement. That he preferred to spend time on other matters was his choice, although they must be seen together enough to persuade everyone—except Felix—that they were happy that they were about to be wed.

A motion in the distance caught her attention. Rising to her knees, she bumped her head against the greenery that was draped along this window as it was at every window in Cheyney Park. She pushed the holly and pine aside as she watched the rider who was headed straight for Cheyney Park's gate. The glitter of sunshine off his golden hair told her that it must be Timothy.

"He rides very well," came a rumbling voice from behind her.

Serenity tried to turn to face the earl and nearly collapsed onto the cushions of the window seat. He put his hand out to steady her as he sat beside her.

"Timothy has been riding across these moors all his life," Lord Brookindale said with a smile. "Sometimes I think he has these winds in his blood. The few times I have visited him in Town, he seemed somehow less alive."

"You may be right." What else could she say? She knew nothing about what Timothy was like in London.

"But he will become as grim as a countinghouse clerk peering along his row of numbers if he continues to work as he has since he arrived at Cheyney Park."

"Work? So that is what he has been doing?"

The earl chuckled and patted her arm. "I have seen your curiosity, young lady, so I know you have wondered where he has been taking himself off to while you have been imprisoned in the care of that arrogant Frenchwoman." He sighed, and his smile fell away. "He thinks I don't know what he is up to. I know the work he does overseeing the building of my factories invigorates him nearly as much as these winds."

"You may be right about that, too." Again she was at a loss for an answer. She wished she had had a chance to learn more about this man she was supposed to be in love with. Hoping she was not choosing the wrong response, she added, "He seldom talks to me of such things."

"Really? You have an obvious intelligence, Serenity, that I have not come to associate with the maids who set upon the Season in search of a husband. I would have guessed that he had regaled you with all the details of his work. If—" His forehead furrowed as he scowled. "Or mayhap I spoke too hastily."

Even though she was certain of so little, Serenity knew the earl was avoiding speaking of something that unsettled him. She wanted to ask what, but again feared that to ask would reveal how little she knew of Timothy.

He heaved himself to his feet. "I think I shall have a few words with my grandson about this. If you will excuse me, Serenity . . ."

She replied, but doubted if he heard her as he strode along the hall, looking as hale as any man two decades younger. Although she wanted to draw her knees up and sit and ponder his words, she resisted that temptation. She needed to get answers for her questions, and only one person could give them to her.

Timothy.

Serenity pushed herself to her feet and hurried along the hall. It took her only a few steps to realize she had no idea where she was in the massive house. While she had walked here from her rooms, she had been so lost in silly thoughts that she had paid no mind to her route. The earl was nowhere in sight, and she did not know which corridor to take to lead her back to where she should be.

Slowing, she decided the best thing to do would be to look out a window and use the outer wall to tell her where she was within the house. She had not seen the full length of the wall, so she hoped this would work.

The first door she tried was locked, as was the next. On the other side of the hall, her luck was no better. She wondered if this was a wing that had been closed off. Odd then that the earl would have been here.

Her eyes widened when she saw a door that was ajar. Opening

it wider, she peered in to see what looked like a child's room, for it had a small bed, several chairs, and a bookcase filled with books. No toys were visible anywhere except for one doll on the bed.

"Who are you?"

Serenity flinched at the demanding question, then smiled at a child who was perched in a chair that seemed far too big for her delicate frame. Glancing around the room, she wondered why such a small child had been left alone. "I am Serenity Adams." For once, she did not stumble on the name. Mayhap she was becoming accustomed to it.

"Are you the Serenity Adams my uncle Timothy is marrying?"

"Yes." That question sounded too mature for such a tiny child. She sat on a chair beside the child. "And who are you?"

"I am Theodora."

"Timothy is your uncle?"

"Not really, but I call him my uncle. My mother is his cousin, twice removed."

Serenity fought to hide her bafflement. This little girl looked no bigger than a six-year-old, but she spoke with the confidence of an older child. She used her left hand when she spoke, but her right one rested in her lap, never moving.

"You have a big family," she said, knowing she must say something to Theodora.

"I guess so." She looked back out the window.

Serenity followed her gaze to see that Theodora had a perfect view of what must be the house's water garden. A pool glittered icy blue amid the snow. It was surrounded by follies that might be buildings or simply facades to enhance the flowers that must grow there in the spring.

"I have not seen you before," Serenity said.

Theodora looked at her. "That is because you have not come here before."

"This is my first visit to Cheyney Park; you are right."

"No, I meant *here*." She tapped the arm of her chair. "I don't go anywhere else."

The child must be jesting. Mayhap she shared Timothy's sense of humor. Not wanting to be caught accepting a falsehood, Serenity asked carefully, "Are you restricted to this room because you misbehaved?"

"Of course not!" Theodora gave her a glance that could be described only as withering. It certainly made Serenity want to crumple up in a ball. "How could I misbehave when I have no chance to?"

"Now you have confused me."

Raising her chin, she brushed her hand against the ribbons on the front of her simple dress. "No one has told you about me?"

"Not a word."

"Oh."

Serenity smiled, but her curiosity gnawed at her. "Will you tell me about you?"

"There is little to tell. I cannot walk, and this hand," she said, pointing to her right hand, "does not work."

"So you sit here all day?" She clasped her hands together to keep them from quivering with her sudden anger. A child should not be left to molder alone in this empty wing of the house simply because she could not walk.

"I cannot do anything else."

"But you could go outside. Someone could carry you." The child was so delicate that Serenity guessed she could carry her easily herself.

"Mama does not want me to chance taking a chill."

"Is your mama here? I would be glad to speak with her."

She shook her head. "Mama prefers to spend winters in Italy." She lowered her eyes. "Of course, the ocean voyage would be too exciting for me in my condition, so I cannot go with her."

"Are you ill?"

Theodora scowled. "I told you that—"

"I know. Your arm does not work, and your legs don't hold you, but are you ill?"

"Like sick with a fever?"

Serenity nodded.

"No."

"Then you should be able to go outside and enjoy the snow."

"Mama is afraid I will take a chill and become sick."

"How about in the summer. Does your mama come here in the summer?"

"Sometimes."

Serenity's heart threatened to break, even as rage boiled in her. How dared Theodora's mother turn her back on her child! Knowing she should not judge a woman she had never met, she still could not submerge all her fury.

She must say something that would not upset the child. "You are lucky that this room gives you a lovely view of the water garden."

"It is much prettier in the summer, when the flowers are out and the ducks take their ducklings for a walk up the hill."

"Lots of ducklings?"

Theodora wore the condescending expression only a child could don in the company of an adult who was treating her as if she were a baby. "They usually have four or five ducklings for each nest."

"I did not know that."

"I have watched, and so I know."

"I am sure you do." She clenched her hands again, then loosened her grip before Theodora took notice of her anger. This poor child had had little else to do but sit here and watch the ducks.

Serenity remained talking with the little girl until the child's nurse, who looked no older than her abigail, Nan, came in. The nurse either did not know how to answer Serenity's questions or chose not to answer, telling Serenity that she must speak with the earl before calling on Miss Theodora again. The child must be closely monitored so that she was not overwhelmed and did not take ill.

Wanting to tell the nurse that the only threat to Theodora was boredom, Serenity held her tongue. She must not jump to conclusions, especially when she had nothing to base her opinions on, save this general disquiet about the whole of the way the child was being treated.

Her Vexation carried her along the hallway until she realized she knew where she was. The portraits of the Cheyney Park ancestors glowered at her, and she glowered back.

"You will not make them smile, no matter how many faces you make at them," Timothy said as he walked toward her.

Crossing her arms so she did not reach out and shake him, Serenity demanded, "Do you know all about Theodora's situation? How can you be a party to it? Don't you have the least bit of compassion for that poor child? If—"

"Whoa," he said, chuckling as he raised his hands in surrender. "One accusation at a time, please."

Serenity took a deep breath, then released it. *Bother!* Why did he have to look so handsome with his face still reddened from the wind and his hair tousled back by his ride across the moors? Her fingers wanted to brush that vagrant strand back and slip along his roughly chiseled face.

"I met Theodora," she said, clamping her arms even closer to her to resist that temptation.

"That much I understood."

She looked away from his scintillating smile. She did not want to let him woo her anger away until she said all that she must. "The way she is being made to sit like an old tough chaperoning a rout is absurd."

He put the tip of his riding boot on the very toe of her slipper as he drew her arms out of their stern pose. "Crossed arms and a tapping foot show me that you are in a pelter, Serenity. No need. No one is trying to abuse the child. We are simply grateful that she has survived this long. The doctors did not believe she would live until her first birthday."

"But what type of life is it for a child to sit in a chair and do nothing save for staring out the window all day? Can she read?"

"She can, but it is easier to read to her, because she cannot hold a book and turn its pages."

She scowled. "She has the use of one hand."

"Some use of it. That is all. The books close when she tries to turn the pages or fall from her lap."

"I refuse to believe that no one can do something for her."

His hands slid along her arms so his fingers could lace through hers. "I chose the wrong name for my betrothed. There is nothing serene about you."

"Don't try to change the subject." She scowled up at him. "Can you devise something to help her?"

"I don't know."

"Will you try?" She tightened her fingers around his as she leaned toward him. "Timothy, I know you are very busy with the plans for your grandfather's party and the many calls you need to make and receive while you are at Cheyney Park."

"You need not make me sound so heartless." Without releasing her hand, he ran the back of his own along her cheek. "Such fire you have! You must have been a vexing scold to your lady."

"I hope I was if she did something as misbegotten as letting a delightful child let her life slip away."

"Your point is well-taken." He hesitated, then asked, "Why is this so important to you?"

"She is a little girl all alone in that empty wing."

"I can understand why that would bother you, but, Serenity, I have never seen you in such a snit. You were ready to banish me to perdition without giving me a chance to explain that I share your dismay, as does my grandfather."

"Then why—"

"We have no choice but to follow her mother's wishes."

"What of Theodora's wishes? She is not a baby any longer. I would wager she is almost six."

"Actually she will celebrate her tenth birthday in the spring."

"Ten?"

Timothy sighed. "The doctors have said that her lack of growth is part of her whole condition. As I said, she was not expected to live at all."

"Then that is an even greater reason to make the time she has more precious and filled with joy."

"All right, Serenity. I will try to devise something to help her read her books."

"Thank you." She smiled and let her shoulders drop from their angry pose. "And I should thank you again for the wonderful clothes that Madame DuLac has been designing for me."

He raised her hand and twirled her about beneath it. Chuckling, he said, "I had heard she was a true mistress of her art of stitchery, but you are the proof. This gown is lovely."

"It is, is it not?" She plucked at the pale pink gauze over the underskirt, then looked up at him. "Timothy, you have ordered more than I will need, even for the time between now and Christmas. What shall you do with all these clothes when this is over?"

"Me?"

"A lady's maid has no use for such elegant clothes."

"No, a lady's maid would not." He frowned.

"What is wrong?"

He shook his head. "Nothing but the course of this conversation. The clothes are for you, Serenity. You may wear them or give them away or sell them, if you wish, but I do not take back gifts."

"They must be so costly. With Madame DuLac and her girls here and—"

"Do not fret over what I am not fretting about."

She wanted to protest again, but saw the unmistakable glint of determination in his eyes. He would not be swayed. She had seen that in his conversations with his cousin and with Mrs. Scott. Even though he might assume a teasing tone, only a widgeon would assume he was ready to cede his will.

Quietly, she repeated, "Thank you."

"You are the one who should be thanked." He tipped her hand over and brushed it with his lips.

She gasped as sensation exploded within her as strongly as had the pain when she woke in the inn. This was far from pain, for it was an exquisite pleasure that had no name.

His eyes grew wide as he slowly lowered her hand away from his lips. Was he astonished, too, at this unexpected burst of delight?

"Serenity . . ." he whispered.

Consternation riveted her. She was not his dream woman. She was . . . Tears seared her eyes, but she raised her chin to keep them from falling. She did not know her name; that was true. Yet she was a person, not a figment of his imagination, created to betwattle his grandfather and offer him pleasure.

Pulling her hand out of his, she backed away one step, then another. He called her name, but she did not stop as she fled along the hall. She did not know where she was going, for she had no idea where she had been. All she knew was that she must not become accustomed to this life, for it could never be hers.

Never.

EIGHT

*T*imothy's ears still rang with the greetings from his effusive Aunt Ilse. He had been squeezed in a bear hug and given an enthusiastic buss on the cheek before he managed to step aside and let Felix receive the same. No guilt pinched him that he had rushed away while Aunt Ilse was treating Melanda Hayes to an identical greeting. It had been easy to disappear when the foyer had been filled with Aunt Ilse's bags and several crates that were as big as a chair. Although he wondered what Aunt Ilse had brought from the Continent on this trip, he did not let his curiosity trick him into staying.

Hurrying down the stairs to the kitchen that opened out into the lower gardens behind the house, he began to doubt if he had heard Mrs. Scott correctly. What would Serenity be doing in the kitchen? He could not guess, for he knew so little about this pretty lady who plagued his thoughts.

Laughter and the clatter of pans and metal utensils greeted him at the wide door that led into the kitchens. This maze of rooms beneath the house had been a favorite place during his childhood, but he seldom came here now. He was not certain when his visits had dwindled or why. They simply had.

Walking into the kitchen, he pretended not to notice how the workers paused and stared when he passed by. Had it been that long since the last time he had come down here? He nodded to them and continued through one room to another, where the aroma of mincemeat and spices reminded how few days were left before Christmas Eve and his grandfather's birthday.

And saying good-bye to Serenity.

That thought made his voice harsher than he had intended when he stopped by a table where Serenity was rolling out dough for a pie. "What are you doing in the kitchen?"

Serenity's eyes widened, and he was overpowered anew by their crystal warmth in the moment before they became icy cold. Looking back at the table, she pinched the crust of one of the pies in front of her as juice oozed out of it. "I enjoy cooking very much, it seems. Apparently I have some true talent in that direction, because your grandfather's cook, Mrs. Gray, has allowed me to work here."

"I thought you were a lady's . . . a lady." He gulped so loudly that one of the kitchen maids turned to stare at him in amazement.

"What I am does not mean that I cannot have talents of various types." She pointed to the trio of pies in the middle of the table. Each was topped with crust cut to look like leaves of holly. "And it seems that I have a true gift for making pie crusts."

"A very good skill to have at this time of year."

"Yes."

When she added nothing else, Timothy hesitated. This conversation had not gotten off to a good start. He tried to recall if any of their conversations had. Clasping his hands behind him, he knew that exchanging heated words with her could lead to even more heated yearnings, the very yearnings that pleaded with him to find a way to speak with her alone again. An endless spiral of risk and need was tightening around him until he was breathless when his gaze met her silvery one.

"My Aunt Ilse has arrived," he said.

Serenity smiled. "So I have heard. Is that why you came down here?"

"No, I was looking for you before I got waylaid in the foyer by Aunt Ilse and her exuberant homecoming."

"I heard she brought a dozen dogs with her."

"Only a rumor." He laughed and leaned one hand on the table. "She has only three. They simply seem like a dozen when they are racing about the grounds. Grandfather has forbidden her to allow them in the Chinese garden, because last year they dug up all the plantings."

"I am surprised he allows her to bring them back."

He shrugged. "I think he is feeling a little guilty for arranging her marriage to that humorless German."

"Guilty? Is that something everyone in your family enjoys wallowing in?" She wiped her hands on her apron. "You act too guilty all the time."

"That is because I feel guilty all the time." He rubbed his forehead with two fingers.

With a laugh, she took a cloth from the table and handed it to him. He regarded her with a baffled expression. Taking the cloth back, she brushed it against his forehead. "You should take care that you do not have flour on your fingers before you start painting your face with it."

"The last time I helped in this kitchen, I was young enough that Mrs. Gray made sure I did not make a mess of myself."

"My lord!" called the cook, as if he had called her name. "Did you wish to request something special for tomorrow's dinner?"

He turned to see Mrs. Gray, who was so gaunt that one would suspect that she hated food and everything to do with it. He knew better, because he had seen her eat with the enthusiasm of a field worker from a plate with enough food to daunt even a growing lad.

Smiling, he replied, "I simply am paying a call upon your domain, Mrs. Gray. It smells wonderful in here."

"You can thank Miss Adams for that." She wiped her hands on her apron, which was stained with every color of food that would appear on the table tonight. "I hope that after you are wed, my lord, you do not feel that you need to give me my congé."

"Why would I ask you to leave?"

"You are getting yourself a wife whom, if she were one of the village lasses, I would have asked to join my staff straightaway." Her smile broadened, stretching her thin cheeks. "Anytime you want to help as you have today, Miss Adams, you are more than welcome."

"Thank you."

Timothy chuckled when a pretty blush caressed Serenity's cheeks as he wished his fingers were. His laugh threatened to strangle him when that craving to hold her exploded inside him. While Mrs. Gray waved an admonishing finger at him and warned him that there would be no samples before the pies were served, he forced a smile. The only thing he wished to sample was Serenity's mouth.

As Mrs. Gray went to check that her cooks were preparing the food just as she wanted, he reached under his coat. Then, looking at the flour covering the table, he asked, "Are you finished, Serenity?"

"Almost. Just this one to go." She placed the pastry in the pie pan and reached for the ladle to pour into it some of the mincemeat that had been prepared, on Stir-Up Sunday at the beginning of Advent. With quick, skilled motions, she set the top crust on it and sealed the edges closed.

"Allow me," he said, as she reached for a knife. He cut the vents in the top of the crust. With a chuckle, he ran his finger along the flat of the blade and wiped off the mincemeat. He licked his finger. "My favorite part of working in the kitchen."

"Just don't let Mrs. Gray see that. She would not want anyone to get the idea that sampling is all right in her kitchen."

He set the knife on the table. "One of the rights of lord of the manor."

"And how many seigneurial rights do you claim, my lord?"

"I am afraid the right of the lord of the manor to share the bed of a bride on her wedding night has long gone out of style at Cheyney Park." Realizing that Serenity was not the only one listening to his answer, he slipped his arm around her waist and tugged her against him. "Save for his own bride."

His breath caught in his throat as her pliant breasts pressed against him. Her eyes grew round, then softened with a luminescence that sent that fiery craving through him again. *Blast it!* He was addled to hold her like this when he wanted to hold her more intimately, to taste the luscious flavor of her mouth, to watch her eyes close as she offered those lips and more to him.

Her fingers coursed across his chest as she whispered, "What is this?"

"What . . .?" He shook the tendrils of longing from his head and smiled as he realized her hand was on the pocket beneath his coat. "That is what I came to show you before I took it to show to Theodora."

"To help her read?"

Again he was aware of the many ears cocked in their direction. A man should not be speaking of a device to help a child when he held the woman he intended to marry in his arms. "Can we go where we can speak more privately?"

"Where?"

He smiled as he released her and held out his hand. "Leave that to me."

Serenity stared past the door Timothy opened at the top of the third floor. This must be Cheyney Park's nursery. Toys were scattered about the room as if a child had been playing with them only that morning. She wondered why Theodora had her rooms below, but she did not ask. The child was isolated too much already.

As she went to peek out the curved window at the moors undulating toward the horizon, she sat on the window seat. This had the same view as the seat where she had spoken with the earl two days ago. In front of the house a trio of wagons were being emptied.

"Aunt Ilse's boxes," Timothy said as he looked past her, leaning his hand on the side of the window, which, unlike the others on the lower floors, was not bedecked with greenery. "She does not believe in being without anything she might need when she comes home."

"Why does not she leave items here for her next visit?"

"You are too logical, Serenity." He laughed. "Aunt Ilse likes to make a grand and glorious entrance wherever she goes. I thought it was because she was a princess, but Grandfather tells me she has been like this since the day she was born."

"Mayhap she knew she was born to be a princess." Folding her hands on her knee, she asked, "What did you want to show me?"

She knew she had spoken unwisely when his eyes glittered like the sun on the snow below. Her fingers curled upon her knees as he reached to draw back his coat. Had he brought her up here to seduce her? She should have guessed what he wanted to "discuss" with her when he whispered softly to her that he wished for them to be alone.

"This." On her lap, he placed a twisted piece of metal with a wooden knob on one end.

"What is it?" she asked, shaken. By her fearful anticipation of his seduction or by her remorse that he was being a gentleman even while she had the most unladylike thoughts of him kissing her?

"Something that I hope will help Theodora read her books." He knelt beside her. "Hold out your hand. It is larger than hers, but I made this somewhat adjustable, because I did not want to get her hopes up needlessly." He smiled up at her. "Or yours before I had some idea it might work."

He latched the metal to her hand with short pieces of leather. The metal device was about as long as her forearm. Standing, he went to a shelf and took down a book. He opened it and set it on her lap. When the book started to close, she put out her hand to hold it in place.

"All right," he said, an intense expression on his face. "Try it. You cannot use your other hand."

"How?"

He reached over and guided her arm so that her elbow still held one side of the book open while the wooden knob reached under the next page. "Now draw it back."

She tried, but the page continued to slip off. Even twisting her arm at a nearly impossible angle did not help. "Mayhap, with some practice, Theodora can manage it."

"If you cannot, she will not be able to either." He tilted her arm so he could examine the page-turner. "What it needs is something to grip the pages, almost like another hand."

"Or fingers."

"Exactly." Standing, he took the book and set it back on the shelf.

She ran her finger along the metal shaft. "But I think you have the right idea. With a few changes, this will be wonderful. You are quite clever, Timothy."

"If I were truly clever, I would have figured out a way to make it work the first time." He chuckled as she struggled with the straps. "And I would have made it easier to take off and put on. Let me help." He undid the leather straps. "That is part of my next challenge. I need to figure out a way that she can take it off and put it on without assistance, but I am going to focus on helping her turn the pages first. I can worry about the other things later."

"She is going to be so excited when you make it work."

"If I do."

"*When.* Look how close it comes to working now."

"Close," he said with a sigh, "is not good enough."

"But it was only your first try."

He held up both hands, his fingers spread wide. "That is actually my tenth try. It seems I finally got the metal part of it right. Now for the gripping part."

"She will be so thankful when you have this all set that it will not matter how many tries it took."

"She has you to thank, Serenity. If you had not chided me, I would not have guessed that Theodora was not perfectly happy in her room."

Serenity took the page-turner and examined the polished wooden knob. "She may be, but that is because she does not know any better."

"I would ask you if you always try to save the world, but I know that is something you cannot answer."

"Mayhap I just have picked up that habit since I woke after the accident."

His brows rose. "You certainly saved me from ruining Grandfather's celebration."

Serenity put the piece of metal on the window seat beside her. Speaking of the lies that she had helped make partly true unsettled her more with each passing day. Her hopes that her memories would come back to her as quickly as the pain vanished had been for naught. Every day there were tantalizing flashes of things she could not quite recall, but nothing came clear.

Not looking at Timothy, she asked, "Was this your room when you were a child?"

"Yes, before I grew old enough to get rooms on the lower floor. Felix was here often, but when he was not, this was my private lair high up near the attics."

"You did not need to worry about suffering from ennui here. There are so many wonderful toys."

He wagged his finger at her as Mrs. Gray had at him. "I know what you are thinking. You are wondering why some of these toys are not downstairs with Theodora."

"Exactly."

"Theodora's mother, my cousin Christina, forbade it. She was worried that—"

"It seems to me that if she was so worried about her child that she has consigned her to sit so she will not hurt herself, she would not leave Theodora here while she winters in Italy and would not come to see her daughter only occasionally."

He sighed. "Don't judge Christina that hard. I own that she is not the best of mothers. Partly it has been because she could not forgive herself for not giving birth to a perfect child. Partly it has been because her husband could not forgive her for that either. And lastly, it is partly because she is more interested in her Italian paramour than anything or anyone else."

"And he does not know about Christina's child."

"Now you understand."

Serenity shook her head. "I don't understand an iota of it. Theodora is an intelligent child." She touched the metal device again. "While you have been putting this together for the past two days, I have been giving Theodora a look-in each afternoon. She has a wit that makes me laugh, and she has a hunger to see more of the world than what she can through that one window."

"Christina has forbidden—"

"That is absurd! How can she be making such commands when she is not here to see what her child needs? If I spoke with your grandfather, he might listen."

"Don't be so certain of that."

"I shall not be." She smiled. "That is why I shall have all my arguments ready for him to listen to."

He laughed and shook his head. "I see you are going to continue to keep things from becoming serene around here."

"You are the one who gave me that name, not me."

"And what name would you have given yourself?"

She started to answer, then sighed. "I don't know."

When Timothy cursed lowly, she knew he had not expected her to hear his oaths. She wanted to assure him that she did not blame him for his playful question. It was not his fault that she could not remember her past enough to guess what she might have been called before he asked her to become his Serenity Adams.

Picking up a rag dog, Serenity said, "This is well loved."

"I think it was the very first toy I was ever given," he replied.

"You certainly received many more."

"Enough to fill this whole nursery. Each New Year's morn, I would leap out of bed and run down the stairs to see if any gifts awaited me." He smiled as he sat on the floor, tucking his feet beneath him as he must have done when he was the child who owned all these wonderful toys. "The anxiety was eased a bit, because on Christmas Eve, Grandfather would put aside the gift I had made him for his birthday, so he could tease me about how he had to open his before I could open any of mine. Then he would open it Christmas morn and let me pick one gift to open that day, too."

"Which was your favorite gift?"

"That I gave him or that he gave me?"

"Both."

He smiled. "All right. Both are easy to answer."

"Your favorite gift from him first."

"This." He pulled a box out of a cubbyhole along the wall and opened it. Spilling its contents onto the floor, he picked up several of the blocks and set them atop one another. "I spent hours building all sorts of structures with these." As he put another block on the stack, he said, "My favorite gift I gave my grandfather was a clock that I had made myself."

She pulled a pillow from the pile on the window seat and set it between her and the sharp mullions on the window. Leaning back, she asked, "You made a clock?"

"Yes. I think I was about twelve." He gave her a sheepish grin. "Of course, I took apart one of the antique clocks to see how a clock worked before I put mine together."

She laughed. "What did the earl say?"

"He thanked me for my gift and then asked when I would be able to pay him for the repairs to the old clock. I did weeks of chores in the stable to pay for that. It taught me to consider the consequences before I made a decision." He paused as he was putting another block in place. "Apparently it did not teach me well enough, or I would not have needed to drag you into all this."

Serenity put the pillow aside and set herself on her feet. Taking care that her dress did not brush the blocks, she crossed the room to where a rocking horse was hidden under a dusty sheet. She drew back the sheet and touched the horse's head. The creak that came from the rockers was the only sound in the room.

"I think you did consider the consequences, Timothy. Otherwise you would never have agreed to the offer Felix made to me. You did not want to hurt your grandfather by showing him that you had been false with him."

"Or maybe I was just determined to do anything to avoid taking the blame for my out-and-outers." He dropped the blocks back into the box. Putting it away, he stood. "You have been very careful not to lay the blame for this at my feet, where it so obviously belongs."

"I need not. You know the truth."

"I know that I could not renege on the offer Felix had made you to help your brother and sister."

Her brother and sister! When had she last given them any thought? Like the rest of her life before the accident, they seemed nebulous and unreal.

"Have you heard anything of them?" she whispered.

"Not yet, but I expected it to be at least a fortnight before I would hear from London." His mouth tightened into the caricature of a smile. "There are so many things and places that need to be checked."

"Are there that many schools?"

"Apparently so."

Serenity closed her eyes. "I know I must have patience, but I know as well that if my brother and sister are found, they will be able to tell me of the past that I have lost."

"And you will have a family of your own again."

"Yes."

"That is important to you, is it not?"

She nodded. "That is one thing I know with every ounce of my being, something that could not be forgotten unless my heart stopped beating. Family is deeply important to me, just as it is to you. It seems that, in that way, we are very much alike."

"In others, we are very different." He ran a single fingertip along her shoulder to the lace beneath her chin. His finger brought her face up toward his. "A complement and a contrast."

She edged away. "Timothy, there are no others here to be betwattled by our apparent affection."

"That is true." His eyes glittered like dust motes dancing in a sunbeam. "Do you long only for apparent affection? Should I believe the words on your lips or the longing in your eyes when I touch you?"

She gripped his sleeves. "Believe both, for both are the truth."

Cupping her elbows, he drew her back to him. "But you will deny us the pleasure we could share with a single kiss?"

"A single kiss?" She shook her head. "Should I believe the words on your lips, Timothy, or the longing in your eyes that tell me a single kiss is not what you are thinking of?"

"You are a wise woman, and I am witless." He released her and brushed his hand against her hair, smoothing it back from her face. When her breath snagged upon the delight she could not control, he said, "It seems I named you for the wrong virtue, Serenity."

"What would you have named me?"

"Prudence seems a more apt name at the moment."

"On that, we agree again." She turned and walked out of the nursery.

When he did not follow her, she wondered if he was the smarter one, for she doubted if she could have resisted the longing in his voice if he touched her again. She was not sure how she would from now on. She must find a way, because soon, she hoped, she would remember her past, and her present with Timothy would be over.

NINE

*T*imothy heard the laughter as soon as he turned the corner in the long hall that led toward the south wing of the house. The sound was unlike any other laughter in the house, for one voice was childish and the other slid along him like an eager caress.

Serenity . . . He had not had two words alone with Serenity since their discussion in the nursery. Each time he saw her, when he had taken a respite from his work finishing up the paperwork on the new factory and reading the reports on the next project or from trying to make that accursed page-turner work for Theodora, she had been with others—usually with Grandfather as they discussed plans for the Twelfth Night celebration, because the earl seemed as smitten with her as a youth suffering from his first calf love. Timothy understood that all too well.

Theodora's laugh soared along the hall, startling him. He did not recall ever hearing her laugh with such enthusiasm. Mayhap Serenity had been right to chide them all about the child. They had begun to treat her with as much solemnity as if they were at her funeral instead of helping her enjoy the years she had been granted. He had been astonished how Grandfather had heeded Serenity's calm suggestions that Theodora should be included when they were *en famille* at dinner. Even Felix's arguments that no other child that young had ever been allowed to join them for dinner had not kept Grandfather from agreeing with Serenity.

Tonight would be the first test of Grandfather's decision, so Timothy had wanted to be certain Serenity knew what she—and Theodora—faced. He would have to guard his words carefully not to upset the child, who must be excited about the unexpected privilege.

The laughter drew him along the hallway. He stood in the doorway, not daring to move. Serenity was sitting on the floor, papers scattered around her. A few strands of her black hair had fallen from the single braid that bound it down her back. They framed her face, accenting its heart shape. Sitting as she was, her gown, a sedate green the same shade as the holly hanging from the window, revealed her ankles and a hint of the slender legs above. His fingers recalled those enticing curves as he had carried her from the carriage and again here up to her rooms upon their arrival.

"Yes, that is right," Serenity said as she folded the page again, drawing his attention back to her face and her smile that set it aglow. "Watch. Now I am going to fold it four more times." She smiled at Theodora.

"When can I cut it?" Theodora asked, her voice buoyant with anticipation.

Timothy frowned. Was Serenity out of her mind? The child could not lift both hands. Serenity would be deranged to think the child would be able to manage the folded sheet and a pair of scissors.

"Just a minute." Serenity chuckled. "There. That last fold is always the toughest." Picking up a pair of scissors from the floor, she knelt beside Theodora's chair. She put the folded page beneath her knee to keep it from opening and reached for Theodora's left hand.

Timothy did not dare to breathe as Serenity curled Theodora's fingers around the handles of the scissors and then held them there with her own hand. Drawing the piece of paper out from beneath her knee, she held it between the open scissors.

"Where first?" Serenity asked, smiling at Theodora.

Although he could not see Theodora's face, he could hear her smile. "Top on your side."

"Top right," she replied. "Big cut or small one?"

Theodora laughed with more excitement than he had ever heard from the child. "Big one. Please, a big one, Serenity."

"All right. Hold tight. I am going to need your help to cut through all of these layers."

The sharp snip of the scissors was loud in the room. Theodora's giggle was followed by more orders of where she wanted Serenity's assistance to cut into the folded paper. When Serenity set the scissors on the floor, she looked toward the door.

"Are you going to lurk there or come in?" she asked.

"Who is it?" Theodora cried.

"Your Uncle Timothy." Serenity motioned gracefully toward the door and smiled. "He has been watching you cut out your first snowflake."

Timothy came into the room and sat cross-legged on the floor beside a stack of white paper. "Snowflakes?" He picked up a handful of white specks that had fallen from her scissors. "These?"

"No." Serenity unfolded the piece of paper she held. "This."

"It's beautiful!" cried Theodora, her eyes wide as she stared at the design that was echoed over and over. The small cuts had created the facets of the snowflake.

"Serenity, that is quite incredible," echoed Timothy. "You did that simply by folding a page and making those snips out of it?"

Kneeling beside Timothy, Serenity sat back on her heels as she folded another slip of paper. "The best thing is, like real snowflakes, no two are alike. I thought we would make some to hang in the windows, so when the guests come for the earl's birthday party, they will see the house all decorated for Christmas."

"You are going to hang them?"

"Actually I thought I would have one of the footmen do that."

"Not me?"

Theodora laughed again when he twisted his face into a pout. "Do you want to be part of our snowflake decorating, Uncle Timothy?"

"I cannot imagine anything I would enjoy more than sitting and chatting with the two prettiest ladies in Cheyney Park while we make snowflakes that I can hang in the windows." He glanced at the ceiling. "And a few here so you can pretend you are sleeping in a snow den."

"A snow den?" Theodora's eyes widened again. "Like a bear hibernating?"

"You may hibernate if you want to miss your great-grandfather's party and all the fun of Christmas," Serenity said with a smile. She glanced at Timothy and saw his smile waver. Sweet heavens, she could not believe that the family would leave this darling child here alone while the rest of them gathered together. Mayhap it would depend on how this evening's meal went. Now was not the time to speak of that, for she did not want to upset Theodora.

"Can he help, Aunt Serenity?" Theodora continued, clearly oblivious to Timothy's reaction. "Please?"

"Can I, *Aunt* Serenity?" Timothy asked with a chuckle.

Serenity handed him a piece of paper to hide her flush of pleasure at his teasing. Her own family was lost to her, and she loved being considered a part of this one, despite all its oddities. Mayhap she had misread his expression. After all, peculiar as it might seem, Theodora knew him better than she did.

"How could I say no?" She laughed, letting her dismay sift away. "It will be amusing to watch you hang what we cut."

He picked up the single snowflake. "Shall I start with this one?"

"Yes!" Theodora clapped her hand against the arm of the chair, her face pink with excitement.

Serenity put her hand on Theodora's knee to calm the little girl. Now she was not mistaking Timothy's expression, for she shared his disquiet. "While Timothy has a ladder brought, you and I can make more snowflakes."

"An excellent idea." He stood. Putting his hand on Serenity's shoulder, he said, "I trust you will have several of these done by the time I return."

"Enough to make a whole den," Theodore replied.

"So many?" he asked, his fingers stroking Serenity's shoulder.

"You may be surprised," Serenity said.

His finger curled up along her cheek. "I find that I always am."

She gazed up at his smile. Nothing she did, no matter how much she avoided being with him, made any difference. Each time they were together, whether alone or with others, even the most chaste touch suffused her with pleasure. She wanted to stand as he pulled her into his arms and up against his strong chest.

When he walked out of the room, she stared down at her hands. They tingled with the longing to touch him, even as casually as he had touched her.

Serenity shook that beguiling thought from her mind when Theodora begged to make another snowflake. Keeping her hands busy would be the best way to prevent them from giving in to her yearning. As she laughed with Theodora, she concentrated on creating pretty designs to please the little girl.

"Will Miss Hayes be at dinner this evening?" Theodora asked suddenly.

"Yes, I believe so. She and your cousin Felix and Aunt Ilse all should be there, too."

"Will you sit beside me?"

"Of course, and your great-grandfather will, too."

"And Timothy will sit beside you." She giggled when Serenity unfolded another snowflake. "Nurse tells me that you and Uncle Timothy like to kiss. That is why you want to get married."

"Why did she tell you that?"

"I asked." Theodora grinned. "I saw Felix and *her* out in the garden kissing, and I asked Nurse about it."

Serenity kept her smile in place as she changed the subject. Making more snowflakes with Theodora's "help" required all her concentration, so again she could put her unsettling thoughts aside. She was no more successful than she had been at trying to put Timothy out of her mind. She had not guessed that Felix and Melanda were anything but friends, because they did not act as if they were in love. It was clear she was mistaken, and why not? How did she know how people in love acted? Mayhap she once had known, but she could not recall.

"Look out!" called Timothy, only a moment before the legs of a ladder came through the door.

Serenity gathered up the paper snowflakes and squeezed in beside Theodora's chair, so she was not struck. "Can you set that up alone?"

"I believe so." He tried to maneuver it through the door.

"Let me help." She guided the end of the ladder past Theodora's bed and toward the floor, so he could set the ladder in place. "Father always called for help with ladders."

"Serenity!" He kicked the ladder open and grasped her arms even as the ladder rocked.

"Father . . ." she whispered.

"What is it, Serenity?" cried Theodora.

Timothy smiled at the little girl. "You know that Serenity lost some of her memories when her head was bumped in a carriage accident, don't you?"

Eyes wide, Theodora nodded.

"Do you remember anything else?" Timothy asked.

Serenity bit her lip as she shook her head. "For a moment I saw a face. My father? I don't know."

"Don't look so distressed. This must be a good sign that you may eventually recall everything."

"I hope so."

"So do I." He winked at Theodora. "What better gift could Serenity receive for the holidays than to remember everything?"

"I would rather have a new doll." Theodora giggled. "One with bright blue hair ribbons."

"Will you settle for a snow den now?"

"Oh, yes!"

Serenity was able to smile sincerely, as Timothy reached under his coat and plucked out some thread. "Where did you find this?" she asked.

"Where else? Madame DuLac was generous."

"And she was busy elsewhere."

"Now you understand." He chuckled as a short man appeared in the doorway. "Ah, Henry, did you find the nails and the hammer we need?"

"I have them right here, my lord." He held out a small wooden bucket. "Good afternoon, miss," he added, tipping his head toward Serenity. "How are you, Miss Theodora?"

"I am going to have a snow den," the little girl said, her eyes twinkling with excitement.

"Are you now?"

Timothy smiled. "Serenity, this is my valet Henry. Henry, Miss Adams."

He dipped his head again. "I hope you are enjoying your call to Cheyney Park, Miss Adams."

"Thank you." Handing a snowflake to Timothy, Serenity said, "This is our prettiest one, so put this where Theodora can see it from anywhere in the room."

Easily Timothy climbed the ladder. He took a nail from Henry and hammered it into the beam running along the center of the ceiling. Tying a thread to it that was as long as his arm, he slipped the other end through one of the cuts in the paper and tied it.

"Perfect!" Theodora craned her neck to try to see the snowflake from another angle. "Look! It sparkles in the sunlight just like real snow.

"You will be surrounded by snow." Serenity knelt to fold another sheet so it could be cut. "We still have a lot more to make if we want to have them for all the front windows, so that all the callers can see them."

She listened to Timothy and Henry discuss with Theodora where to hang the snowflakes. Varying the length of the threads gave the illusion of being in the midst of a gentle storm. She continued to work on the snowflakes, trying to stay ahead of Timothy, so he would not have to wait for the next one.

When Henry brushed some of the scraps of paper away from where she was sitting, she smiled. "Thank you."

"Glad to help, miss." He grinned before helping Timothy move the ladder closer to the door.

"Serenity?" Timothy asked.

"Yes?" She cut another piece out of the page.

"Serenity?"

When she looked up, she laughed as he tossed bits of paper in the air. Theodora crowed with joy as they wafted down around her.

Gathering up a handful as Henry must have, Serenity took Theodora's hand and closed her fingers around the paper. She rose and whispered in the little girl's ear. Theodora compressed the scraps into a wad. With a laugh, she let the paper fly at Timothy. It struck him in the arm.

"What was that?" he asked with a gasp.

"A paper snowball." Serenity laughed while Theodora giggled. "A snowball aimed very well at you!" She squeezed the little girl's hand gently.

Glancing at Henry, he said, "I think we have been challenged to a snowball fight." He jumped down from the ladder and grabbed another handful of scraps. He dumped the paper over Theodora's head. As Theodora shouted for Serenity to gather up more of the white pieces so she could make another snowball to throw at him, he scooped up more of the paper and dropped it on Serenity's hair.

He caught her arm as she was reaching for a piece of paper. She shook it off and crinkled the page into a wad. Throwing it at him, she laughed when it struck him on the chin.

"Now you are asking for it," he said in a growl. Grasping her arm, he sprinkled scraps on top of her head.

She tried to collect more pieces of paper, but he halted her, clamping his arm around her waist and pulling her up against him. The sound of Theodora's gleeful laughter faded in the distance as she gazed up into his eyes. His fingers eased their grip on her arm as his other hand swept up her back, pressing her even closer.

"You are beautiful when you are covered with snowflakes," he whispered. "Your cheeks are flushed, and your hair is soft around us. And your lips look hungry for a kiss to warm them."

"It is not cold in here."

"You are right." His hand stroked her back. "It is very warm with you in my arms."

"Theodora is here." She wondered how she could talk him out of kissing her when she wanted him to so very much.

With a laugh, he looked over his shoulder. "Would you be bothered if I kiss Serenity?"

"Nurse says that is what people who want to get married do." She grinned.

"As you don't mind, and Henry does not mind—"

"Only if Miss Adams does," the valet said with a chuckle.

"Do you mind, Serenity?" Timothy asked quietly. "Do you mind if I savor a sample of your soft lips?"

"You should not—"

"Heed what you say, but what your eyes tell me." His fingers sifted through her loosened hair, sending it cascading along her back.

When he tilted her mouth toward his, she raised her arm to curve around his shoulders. Why was she fighting what she wanted with all her being? His hair, like unrefined silk, brushed her fingers, and his sand-rough face grazed her as he placed a light kiss on her left cheek. When he moved to kiss her other cheek, she caught his face in her hands. His eyes burned like the dark wood at the very heat of the fire, sparks glinting through their ebony.

"I thought you wanted to kiss my lips," she whispered so softly not even Henry or Theodora could hear.

"More than you can know, sweetheart." He bent toward her as anticipation quivered deep within her.

"What is this mess?" came a mocking voice from the doorway.

Serenity yanked herself away from Timothy to see Melanda Hayes in the doorway. The quivers became shivers of dismay that the precious moment had passed when she could have delighted in his kiss.

"*What* have you done to yourself now, Serenity?" Melanda's nose wrinkled in distaste. "I cannot believe that the earl would consider marrying his heir to someone who is so unkempt."

She put her hand up to her hair, which billowed around her with every motion, and replied coolly, "I might find it easier to stay a pattern-card of perfection if I did nothing but sit all day and ply my needle to a piece of fabric." She halted herself before she could say more.

Seeing Melanda's eyes brighten, Serenity knew she would be a widgeon to allow the young woman to send her into a pelter. Melanda Hayes enjoyed an uproar. No quiet meal was allowed. Melanda seemed compelled to prattle about someone she had met in London who did not meet her expectations, delighting in belittling them, especially if they revealed any skills she could never obtain.

Quietly, Serenity continued, "To own the truth, we were having a snowball fight."

"Inside?"

"One does not get chilled this way." She bent and gathered up another handful of the paper scraps. Tossing them into the air, she said, "This is our blizzard." She looked at where Timothy still stood beside the ladder. "Timothy is hanging up some of our snowflakes."

Melanda's nose wrinkled again. "That is so—"

"Amusing," Felix said as he appeared behind her. Resting his shoulder on one side of the doorway, he folded his arms in front of him. "Is this your idea, Serenity?"

"A very good one," Timothy said. He put his hand on Serenity's back, gently stroking it.

Did he think this would help calm her? Mayhap her anger, but his touch sent a pulse through her that set every inch of her to shimmering like the air after a bolt of lightning cut through.

"Will you go away?" Theodora asked with childish candor. Too much candor, Serenity realized, when she went on, "Timothy was about to kiss Serenity."

"Is that so?" Felix's smile grew brittle. "That is a surprise, knowing what I know about you."

Serenity stiffened, but before she could think of what to say, Theodora added, "Why is that a surprise? They are getting married. People who are getting married kiss."

"That is so." Felix squatted by her chair. "You know a lot, don't you, Theodora?"

"I know you and Miss Hayes must be getting married, too."

"Miss Hayes and I have made no such plans." He glanced at Timothy, who was watching without expression, then gave Theodora another smile. "You should not heed what you hear."

"I am heeding what I *saw*. I saw you and Miss Hayes kissing in the water garden."

Felix stumbled back to his feet as Melanda's face blanched. She said something to him that Serenity could not hear while they left the room.

"Henry," Timothy asked in their wake, "will you find Theodora's nurse, please?"

"Yes, my lord." He wore a worried expression. "If I can do anything else, my lord . . ."

"Nothing else. Serenity and I will begin cleaning up this mess with Theodora's supervision while you retrieve Theodora's nurse."

Serenity knelt again by Theodora's chair when she saw tears glistening in the little girl's eyes. "Don't be sad. If you cry, you will melt the roof of your snow den."

"I will, won't I?" Theodora gave her a watery grin. "I did not mean to cause trouble."

"You caused no trouble," Serenity assured her.

"None at all." Timothy handed her some of the paper scraps. "While you make another snowball, I need Serenity to help me pick up more of this paper."

Seeing the intensity in his eyes, Serenity nodded. She was not surprised when he led her to the farthest pieces on the carpet. As she knelt to pick up the white spots that stuck stubbornly to the floor, she whispered, "I am sorry if Theodora unsettled you with her comments about Felix and Melanda. She had mentioned that earlier to me and—"

"My cousin may kiss whomever he pleases, as he always has."

"Then what bothered you?"

He took her hand and dumped the pieces she held into his. "I do not like being threatened, Serenity."

"Threatened?" She grasped his arm. "I had hoped I heard Felix wrong."

"You did not."

She stood when he did. Keeping her voice low, she said, "Timothy, if you want to put an end to this betrothal now, I will do what you need me to do."

"And then what?"

"I don't know."

He put one finger beneath her chin and tipped it toward him. "I shall not have you turned out with no place to go."

"Your house in London—"

"Would mean the ruin of your reputation if it was learned I set you up there. Everyone would assume you were my mistress, and no lady would hire you to work in her household." He smiled coolly, even though his eyes still burned as they had when he had been about to kiss her. "I am not ready to end our betrothal yet, but I am beginning to wonder if my cousin had only our grandfather's best interests at heart when he concocted this plan in that inn."

"But what could he hope to gain otherwise by making sure you remained in your grandfather's favor?"

"I don't know, Serenity, and I hope I am wrong. I do know, however, that I intend to find out."

TEN

*T*imothy closed the accounts book and leaned back in his chair. This latest letter updating the new factory project had been just what he had hoped for. The land was available at a good price, and there were plenty of potential employees who were willing to accept the generous wages that he insisted all who worked for his grandfather be paid.

"If you want the best, you have to be willing to pay for them," he mused. How many times had he said that to himself and others?

"That is why I thought you would be willing to pay so well for your Serenity's assistance." Felix came into the small room that was not much wider than the bay window at its far side. Walking past Timothy's desk, he sat in the room's only other chair.

"I have wondered why you were so generous with my money." Putting the book into a drawer, Timothy stood and stretched. He went to the window. The sun had passed its zenith and was heading toward the western horizon, warning that he had missed the midday meal.

Felix lit a cigar from a brand taken out of the fireplace.

"Mrs. Scott will be distressed to see you smoking around the greenery," Timothy said.

Felix settled back in his chair and tilted the cigar to watch the smoke drift across the room. "Mrs. Scott would not get upset about the greenery getting all scented with smoke if she did not put it up everywhere."

"It is Christmas." Timothy stood by the bay window and looked out over the grounds. It was snowing again. Winter seldom started with such a vengeance here on the moors. The gray sky fit in perfectly with his mood. Not only had every attempt to invent the perfect page-turner for Theodora been an absolute failure, but he wanted to relish that kiss that had been interrupted.

"Where is a man supposed to enjoy a funker when the whole house is bedecked with holly and mistletoe?" He chuckled. "Of course, you have every reason to enjoy having the kissing boughs about. It seems somehow ironic that you did not want to make a jumble of Grandfather's birthday, but you are the one who has received the finest gift."

"What are you babbling about?"

Felix leaned forward, resting his elbows on his knees. "Why, old chap, I am not blind. I see you skulking about the house, seeking any chance to be with your dear Serenity. You are even hanging paper snowflakes from the ceiling, for heaven's sake."

"You are queer in your attic, *old chap*," he said in a snarl, turning to look back out the window.

"Aha!"

"Aha what?" He should not be encouraging a continuation of this conversation, but he preferred anything to his thoughts, which were a mixture of recriminations and cravings. Could Theodora be right about Felix and Melanda Hayes? They had been friends since childhood, so she must know of Felix's philandering ways that took him in and out of the boudoirs of many houses in Town. He could not guess why she would be such a muttonhead as to give her heart to Felix, because he had heard Melanda boast more than once that she would marry only for love or for a grand title. As Felix would never have the family's title, Melanda must have a deep affection for him.

"I recognize that tone." The chair scraped as Felix came to his feet. Crossing the room, he wedged himself between Timothy and the window, so Timothy had no choice but to look at him. "That tone means the point has struck too close to the mark."

"And what mark is that?"

"That you have developed a *tendre* for Miss Serenity Adams."

He shook his head. "Now I know you are deranged. Why would I do something skimble-skamble like that? As soon as the holidays are over, so is this so-called betrothal."

"But that does not mean you cannot be attracted to her."

Timothy smiled coolly. "That is true, and it is true she is a lovely woman with a warm heart."

"'Tis not her heart that you think of warming you."

"Felix, you should not speak so of her."

Felix looked at the ceiling and crowed with laughter. "Are you forgetting that she is not of quality? She is in service, a lady's maid. Who better to offer her services to than you?"

Timothy's hands were on his cousin's lapels before he realized what he was doing. With a curse, Timothy shoved him away. "If you say nothing of this again, I shall forget you said anything of it now."

"Be that as it may," Felix replied, brushing his coat as if Timothy had dirtied it, "you and I may pretend to put this conversation out of our minds, but you cannot put her out of your mind." He laughed sharply. "She is quite taken with you, too, if you have failed to notice."

"I have not." He could not rid himself of the image of Serenity's wondrous eyes so close to his in the moment before hers closed in anticipation of his kiss. It seemed to be seared onto his eyeballs, a ghostly vision of beguilement that followed him everywhere.

"Did you consider that she might want you to show her the course of your thoughts? It appeared she was more than willing when we intruded upon you yesterday."

"I cannot speak of the course of her thoughts." Another lie to add to his list of bangers. He had seen the truth in Serenity's gaze and sensed it in her touch. She knew the danger of succumbing to this temptation, but she was willing to face that risk.

Puffing on the cigar, Felix went on as if Timothy had not spoken, "She would not dare to show you openly how she would like to share more than cutting out fake snowflakes with you, and she probably will push you away if you try to seduce her—the first few times, for she is trying to be a lady. You might not find her as averse as you think in the long run."

"There is no long run."

Felix shrugged his shoulders. "Then you are a fool not to take advantage of what is before you right now. I, on the other hand, have gained the privilege of kissing more than Melanda's hand."

"A gentleman does not speak of these things."

Felix laughed. "A gentleman does not need his cousin to point out the truth that a serving woman is pining for him to pursue her and take her as his special gift for the holiday season."

Timothy started to retort, then walked out of the room. He had no answer. Everything Felix said was true.

"And this is my very favorite painting of the front of the house near the Swiss border." Aunt Ilse's collection of chins bounced with her enthusiasm as she held up the canvas in front of Serenity. "Usually this hangs right over the hearth in the solarium. I love how the sunshine dances off the colors."

"It must be lovely." Serenity bit back the question she wanted to ask. The canvas must be at least two feet wide on each side. Why did Aunt Ilse bring it back and forth to Cheyney Park? Certainly she could have had a miniature of it done.

"Especially in the wintertime, when the sun reflects off the snow. Of course there can be snow on the mountain peaks all summer. It is so lovely there. I seldom come back to England for Christmas, because the holidays are so dreary here. We have so much more fun on the Continent." She leaned the canvas against a table where the previous dozen she had shown Serenity were propped. Taking Serenity's hands in her bejeweled ones, she said, "You and Timothy must spend your wedding trip with Rupert and me. We shall show you all of Europe. It will be such fun."

"I am not sure what Timothy has planned."

Aunt Ilse smiled. "My dear, dear, dear, naïve child. You and I must have some heartfelt discussions. You must learn to let your husband *think* he is making the decisions. Who knows better what a husband should have than his wife?"

"To own the truth, I have thought about no plans beyond this holiday season."

"But you plan to marry before the Season begins."

"Yes, yes, we do." Serenity wondered when Timothy had set a date for their supposed wedding. She wished he would inform her of the tales he was spinning. "Did Timothy tell you that?"

"No, I did." Felix walked into the room, smiling. "I hope it was not supposed to be a secret, Serenity." He chuckled. "If you and Timothy had made plans to run off to Gretna Green, you would be disappointing everyone in the family, for the last big wedding here was yours, I believe, Aunt Ilse."

"I believe you are right." Aunt Ilse brushed back her fading blond hair, which must have been as spectacular as Timothy's when she was a young miss. "That was a stunning day. The sun shone, and the birds sang a special song."

"No one was disappointed that day, as they were when Timothy and Charlene canceled their wedding plans."

Serenity sat straighter, but swallowed her gasp. When she saw Felix's grin, she knew he had come here specifically to let her know this. Timothy had planned to marry before? She thought of the many times he and others had paused in mid-sentence when they spoke of the recent past. Timothy must have invented a fiancée when he wanted to reassure his grandfather that he was doing his best to get the title an heir.

She was saved from answering when a footman came to the door. He bowed and said, "Mr. Wayne, your presence is requested in the foyer."

"A caller?"

"Yes, sir." He bowed again before hurrying away.

Felix offered his arm. "Aunt Ilse, would you like to join me to see who is calling?"

"Delighted, my boy." She rose with a whisper of satin and lace. "I wonder who it could be." Pausing at the door, she asked, "Serenity, my dear, are not you joining us?"

"I thought I might—"

"Nonsense!" Aunt Ilse motioned for her to stand and follow them. "We shall greet this visitor; then I shall have that discussion with you that you must have posthaste. I cannot believe that your mother neglected your education like this."

"My mother died when I was younger than Theodora." Serenity halted in midstep. *That* was the truth, a stitch of memory that somehow had been resewn into her mind. She clasped her hands in front of her as she recalled the day her mother had died. Around her was a sea of black. She could hear weeping and see the raw wound of the opened earth. The sunshine was sparkling off the sea beyond some cliffs where houses were set close together. Yet she could not see a single face or anything to distinguish this village from the hundreds that lined the British coast.

"Serenity?"

At Aunt Ilse's impatient call, Serenity regretfully shook off her thoughts. She did not want to lose these memories again, but they offered her no help now. Hurrying to where they waited, she said nothing as they went down the stairs to meet whomever was waiting in the foyer.

Serenity could not keep from smiling when she saw Timothy below them, just stepping off the lowest step. Nor could she halt her feet from carrying her down the stairs with untoward speed. When he turned, he offered her a smile of his own. He held out his hand, and hers rose to weave her fingers through his. He folded his elbow, drawing her closer.

"I hear we will be stringing berries next," he said with a laugh. "Does Theodora wish to have berries to feed her bear in her snow den?"

"To own the truth, your aunt asked me to help with that."

"Why?"

"I am not sure. She said we all would be pleased to see how she intends to use the strings of berries." She glanced up the stairs. "I thought we would bring Theodora to the parlor later this afternoon and begin the work."

"An excellent idea. Then we show off what we have accomplished at dinner."

The front door opened, sending an icy wind swirling around the foyer. Branson held out his hand for the cloaked man's hat as he greeted him.

Serenity stared. As surely as she had known that bit of memory was of her mother's funeral, she knew she had seen this man before. Again disquiet surged through her, but she was not certain why.

When Timothy drew her forward, he said, "Welcome home, Uncle Arnold." He smiled at her. "Serenity, allow me to introduce my uncle, Arnold Wayne, Felix's father. Actually, to keep you from being confused, I should say my grandfather's nephew. Uncle Arnold, this is Serenity Adams."

"Your betrothed?" asked Mr. Wayne with a broad smile.

"A pleasure, Mr. Wayne," she said, trying to ignore her instinctive yearning to pull her hand away. She was not sure what was causing the uneasiness in her stomach.

Arnold Wayne resembled his nephew more than his son, because he had pale golden hair. It did not have the sheen of Timothy's hair, which seemed to capture the sunlight. His nose was broader, and his eyes seemed to be watching all of them with an odd intensity.

And what was oddest of all was that she was sure she had seen him before. Although she knew that was unlikely, she could not rid herself of that sensation. She had endured it with only one other person—Felix Wayne.

Mayhap they had called at the household where she had been in service. If that were so, she could have seen them when they called, although they would have not taken note of her.

Sorrow cut through her. If Mr. Wayne had recognized her, he might have been able to answer some of the questions that haunted her. The foremost one was her real name. Then she wanted to know why she had glimpses of a mother and a father, but the idea of a brother and sister seemed alien.

Mr. Wayne bowed over her hand. "I am delighted to meet you. I trust you will allow me the informality of family, so I may call you Serenity."

"Of course," she replied, although she wanted to ask, *Have you seen me before?*

"You are every bit as beautiful as Felix led me to believe." He smiled at his son. "You did not tell me that Serenity would be joining us here at Cheyney Park."

"It was a surprise for all of us." Felix chuckled. "But a most pleasant surprise."

"You must tell me all about it while I go up to my rooms and change into something appropriate for dinner." He looked down at his clothes, which were stained with mud. "I had hoped to get here earlier, but the weather is determined to make this celebration an intimate one with only family." He flashed a smile at Serenity. "Or future family."

She smiled back. She could not fault him for her own uncertain memories. Why should she trust a single one of the images that flashed through her head? Even though she believed the ones of her father and mother were true, she could not swear to that.

As Felix and his father climbed the stairs, Aunt Ilse following them and chattering about how much she had to show her cousin, Timothy said, "If we want to get started stringing those berries, we should begin now. Uncle Arnold will want us men to stay late at dinner tonight over port and cigars. He always has many opinions that he likes to air."

"It does not sound as if you agree with all of them," Serenity replied.

"I agree with a few of them some of the time." He grinned as he offered his arm. Leading her up the stairs, he glanced toward the window. "He is right about one thing. If this snow continues to fall as it has, Grandfather's birthday ball will be a very lightly attended one."

"Which may please him."

He paused on the stairs. As she continued up and around the banister at the top, he put his hand on hers. He looked up at her as if she were standing on a balcony and he in the garden below. "You seem to understand my grandfather well already."

"He likes his quiet. I believe he would rather spend his day with a book than anything or anyone else."

"He says often that reaching an advanced age allows him to do as he wishes instead of as society wishes."

She laughed. "I have heard him say that." Biting her lower lip, she hesitated, then asked, "Why, then, are you planning such an assembly to celebrate his seventieth birthday?"

"Because he would be distressed if we did not."

"I don't understand."

He laughed as he stroked her fingers beneath his on the railing. "Neither do I, but that is the way Grandfather is. He has his opinions of how things should be done. His life should be quiet when he wishes it to be quiet. He can have a grand party, although he wants the guests not to disturb him before that hour." His smile faded. "And he wants his heir to have an heir or two of his own before his thirtieth birthday."

"Felix tells me that you had intended to marry."

"Felix has a problem with keeping any secret." Timothy continued up the stairs.

She stepped in front of him to keep him from walking away. "Then why have you taken him into your counsel about all of this?"

"*He* was the one who persuaded you to sell a few weeks of your time for five hundred pounds, if you will recall. I could hardly keep him from knowing about that."

"No, I mean about the letters you wrote to your grandfather about Serenity."

"Actually Felix had a hand in creating Serenity when Grandfather asked for more details about this paragon who I had told him had touched my heart." He shook his head. "At the time it seemed amusing and harmless. I should have known that no lie is ever without hidden dangers."

"Did you lie because you wanted to hide your broken heart?"

His fingers curved along her cheek. "My pride was hurt, I must own. My heart? Not really. Do you know how few of the *ton* marry for love?"

"I have never understood why people who have every other advantage feel it is adequate recompense for a lack of love in their lives."

"You are such a romantic, Serenity."

"I know that *I* would never settle for less than love."

As his fingertip traced along her cheek to the corner of her lips, he said, "You will make some man very happy when you give him your heart."

"As you would make a woman happy, if you would give your heart." She could not believe they were speaking like this when her heart pounded against her breast, demanding to be heard. She must not heed it and its plea to be offered to him. His words made it clear that he considered the proper wife who would give him the proper heirs more important than love. Through all of this, she could emerge with her heart unscathed only if she guarded it well.

"Charlene Pye was a woman I believed I could be happy with all my days, as I thought she would be happy with me." He sighed and locked his hands behind him. "However, she had no interest in sharing me with anything else."

"What anything else?"

"My work."

She frowned. "Forgive me, Timothy, but what work does a viscount do? I have heard Felix speak of nothing more onerous than deciding which cravat to wear when he goes to the theater or to the card table."

"Do not regale me with your lower-class arrogance. What do you know of my life?"

Serenity stared at him in astonishment. He never had spoken to her with such coldness. She had not intended to hurt him with her blunt question, but it seemed she had touched upon something that unsettled him greatly. "Timothy, I—"

"No, you should not apologize." He sighed as he drew her into the parlor where she had been sitting with Aunt Ilse. Closing the door, he said, "I should apologize to you and to my grandfather. You have done all you can to help me, and he wishes only to see me happy and settled with a family of my own. Instead I treat you both as if you are the ones who have created this muddle."

"But what is it that upset you when I asked that question? I did not mean to probe where I should not."

"Why should not you ask anything you wish? I have demanded nothing less of you than to remake yourself in the image of a woman I invented."

She sat on the settee next to Aunt Ilse's paintings. "To be honest, I am grateful for that."

"Really?" He sat beside her. "Why?"

"If I had not been able to become Serenity, I might have been completely lost." She put her hand on his fist, which was balanced on his knee. "Why did you invent Serenity?"

"Because I did not want to be bothered by another fiancée like Charlene Pye. I wanted to be able to concentrate on completing my project." Sliding his other hand over hers, he smiled. "One thing I should tell you, Serenity. I enjoy supervising the building of things."

"I saw that in the nursery."

"What?"

"With the blocks."

He chuckled, the tension leaving his face. "In this case, I was building a factory for one of the textile companies that Grandfather owns. I know a gentleman is supposed to let others deal with such matters, but I like to be part of the creation of something new and wondrous like a factory."

"That would not surprise your grandfather, if you have been this way since you were a child."

"He has been determined that I know a gentleman's duties and obligations."

"But he must have seen how you loved building things with blocks." She smiled gently. "And with clocks." Sympathy rushed through her. Timothy had been so pleased to help with hanging the snowflakes and making the snow den for Theodora. Yet no one in this family considered that gift of good sense as important as finding a suitable wife who would give him sons to continue the family name. No wonder he had created Serenity Adams to placate his grandfather.

"Grandfather knows that I dabble in the work. He does not guess how much time I spend with it." He sighed. "Until now, only Felix knew. Now you do, too."

"Felix knows a lot about you."

"I have seen that you are uncomfortable in his company." When she drew her hand away and stood, he gazed up at her. "I saw as well the peculiar look you had on your face when you met Uncle Arnold."

"He looked familiar to me."

He grasped her hands, folding them between his. "Do you know when you might have seen him?"

"No, and it seems he does not recall me. He said nothing to suggest we had ever met."

"Mayhap he thought you would prefer he not say anything when others were about."

Serenity gasped. "Does he know the truth about this charade?"

"I would not be surprised. Felix and his father are very close." She put her hand on his shoulder. "I am sorry, Timothy."

"Sorry?" He looked up, amazement widening his eyes.

"It must be difficult for you to see Felix with his father and think about what life would have been like if your father had not died."

"I cannot think of that."

"I would." She rubbed her arms as she crossed the room to look out the window, which was draped in holly. Snow drifted past the glass, then whirled in a mad dance as the wind gathered it up and tossed it away. "I know how I look at you when you are with your family, and I think of all I have forgotten. My mother died when I was young."

"You remembered that?"

"Yes, just before we came down to greet your uncle. Do I have any family living other than my sister and brother? Mayhap I have cousins, too."

Setting himself on his feet, he put his hand on her shoulder, then raised it to run it gently against her cheek. "I should have considered that, but I have been wrapped up in my own fretting."

"You did consider that. You wrote to London to find out what you could about my brother and sister."

"And heard nothing." He took in a deep breath, then let it slide past his clenched teeth. "I think 'tis time I jostle Ballard's elbow."

"Ballard?"

"My solicitor. 'Tis time to remind him that you are waiting anxiously for any information he might have garnered during his prowls about Town."

"No matter what it is, I shall not leave before your grandfather's party on Christmas Eve."

"As you promised."

"I know I promised, but I wanted to reassure you on that point." She gave him a weak smile. "My head has been banged up some, but not enough that I would not recall a promise I had made to you."

"I suspect you hold all vows you make most dear."

"Yes." Should she say more? Should she speak of how, when she came down the stairs each morning, she listened for the sound of his voice among all the others? Should she tell him how his touch trilled through her like the first birdsong of spring? "I know how important this is to you."

He turned her slowly to face him. "But do you know how important *you* are to me through all this?"

A knock on the door halted her answer. Clamping her lips closed before the words could tumble out, she threaded her fingers together in front of her as he went to the door. She heard Theodora's nurse's apology for intruding.

Going to the door, Serenity said, "Tell Theodora we will be there posthaste."

Nurse nodded, her ruddy hair bouncing out of its bun, before she turned and rushed toward Theodora's room.

"We have berry strands to make," Serenity added into the silence that was left behind the nurse. "I do not want to disappoint Theodora by making her wait a moment longer."

"But you will disappoint me?"

She backed away a step from the potent need in his gaze, but bumped into the open door. As he closed the distance between them, she gripped the edge of the door to keep her fingers from sweeping up his arms as she invited him to enfold her to him. "Timothy . . ."

"Don't tell me you don't understand what I mean," he whispered. "I can see the truth in your eyes that glow like soft pools of a sunlit sky." His hand raised to cup her cheek, then lowered.

"And I can see, as well, that you are the wiser of the two of us to know that, if I do not wish to disappoint my grandfather, I must be disappointed."

"Yes." She dared say no more, for the entreaty for him to pull her into his arms burned on her tongue.

"You do not say that you are disappointed as well, sweetheart."

Her fingers tightened on the door at the endearment she longed to believe he meant with sincerity. Quietly she said, "I know what I must do and how I must act if I am to have the life I should after this is over."

"And you are gone away?"

She nodded.

"I don't like to think of that time," he whispered.

"Nor do I, but I must."

With a sigh, he stepped back and held out his hand to her. "Let neither of us think of that now. Let's think only of how many more berries I can string this afternoon than you can."

"Do you really think you can best me in stitching them together, Timothy?" She let her voice lighten and saw his lips tilt in the beginnings of a smile. "You may be able to build a fancy factory, but I must have much more experience than you with a needle."

"Shall we see about that?"

She slipped her hand into his, wondering how anything that should not be could be so wondrous. "Yes, we shall."

ELEVEN

What the . . ."

Timothy looked up from where he had been watching Serenity help Theodora thread cranberries and crab apples along a
string that reached from her chair nearly to the hearth in Grandfather's favorite reading room. He laughed when the earl wiped
spots of juice from his face.

"I thought this was supposed to be *dried* fruit," Lord Brookindale grumbled.

"Apparently some of it is not totally dry." Timothy handed his
grandfather a handkerchief. Sitting back on the floor and picking
up his own needle and piece of thread that was almost covered
with fruit, he asked, "How long does Aunt Ilse want this strand
of dried fruit?"

"She said to fill up all the threads." Serenity turned to look
at the lengths of stringed fruit that snaked around the room. "It
appears that we are almost finished."

Theodora chuckled as Serenity held a piece of fruit for her to slip the needle through. "That is good, because we are nearly out of fruit."

"Mrs. Gray told me that this last canister was the final one she could spare unless the household wanted to be without fruit for the rest of the winter." Serenity edged the crab apple closer to Theodora's needle. "Watch out for my fingers!"

"I am trying." Theodora giggled.

Timothy glanced at his grandfather as the earl laughed along with the little girl. Serenity might have come into this household as a stranger, but she was showing those who lived here how to be a family. Since Serenity had brought Theodora to join in family events, there had been a return of his grandfather's gentleness that Timothy recalled from his own childhood.

When his grandfather stood, Timothy came to his feet as well. He followed the earl to the other side of the room and nodded when his grandfather held up a bottle of wine. Taking the glass the earl handed him, he was not surprised when his grandfather said, "You must want to say something very important to me, or you would not have wandered so far from Serenity's side."

"Shall I simply say that I am pleased at how well Serenity has fit into this family?"

"Bah!" Lord Brookindale sniffed his disagreement. "You had no worries about that, for you told me from the onset that she seemed perfect to be your bride."

"Don't confuse optimism with practicality."

"That *I* would never do, my boy." He sat in a chair near the table where the rest of the bottle of wine waited. Looking back at where Serenity was laughing with Theodora, he added, "Tell me what is truly on your mind."

Timothy wished he could obey that order. Yes, the whole of this was going far better than he had had any reason to expect, but he still wished to be honest with his grandfather about the tale he had spun. Swallowing his sigh before it could betray him, he replied, "I am pleased that Serenity has opened our eyes to Theodora."

"Yes, she has." Lord Brookindale's smile dimmed. "She dares to love that child, no matter the consequences."

"That seems to be her way."

"It is a very special way. I know she suspects that the child has been isolated apurpose, and she is not so wrong." He took a drink of his wine, and Timothy noticed that his hands shook. "From the day Theodora was born, we feared she would not survive for long. I have lost so many of those I have loved that I did not want to love and lose another."

"So you gave her that pretty room to die in to ease your guilt and kept yourself distant?"

He nodded. "This is nothing I am proud of, mind you, but it allowed me to forgive her mother for abandoning her and to forgive myself for doing much the same, even though I made sure she had excellent nurses."

"To own the truth, I thought you were doing the best thing for her."

"Then Serenity arrived, and she tipped everything over and inside out." His smile returned as he raised his glass toward Timothy. "Your marriage to her will never been serene, but it should be very interesting and most pleasurable. She is clearly a woman of strong passions, a woman who matches your stubborn nature."

Timothy could not keep his gaze from going to Serenity. On her knees by Theodora's chair, she smiled warmly as she concentrated on holding the cranberry where the little girl could push the needle into it. Then Serenity helped thrust the needle through and held Theodora's hand while they guided the piece of fruit along the string. He guessed Serenity's fingers must be pocked with marks from the tip of the needle, but she had not complained as she made Theodora a part of whatever Aunt Ilse had planned.

Strong passions? That, he believed, was an understatement. Serenity's eyes mirrored her every emotion, each one powerful and a challenge to any man who dared to come close enough to sample them. And sample them was what he wished to do. How she had trembled when he kissed her hand! He longed to hold her in his arms as his lips found hers while she quivered against him.

"A groom-to-be should be besotted with his lady love," Grandfather said with a low rumble of a laugh. "That is why I wanted you to find love instead of dragging you into some silly arranged marriage that would have made you miserable."

"You arranged my parents' marriage, and they were quite happy."

His full brows rose. "Not at first. Your mother thought your father was an insufferable fool, and he considered her to have no thoughts about anything but spending his money." With another laugh, he added, "But they got past that quickly."

"I am glad to hear that."

"I am sure you are! You and Serenity will not have to go through those months of pretending to care about each other during the day and avoiding each other at night." Lord Brookindale glanced again at Serenity. "I would say you might be suffering from quite the opposite."

Timothy folded his hands around his glass. "I have not cuck-olded the parson with her, if that is what you are hinting at, Grandfather."

"I am speaking of your thoughts, my boy, not your actions."

"One's thoughts are seldom easy to control."

"You are beginning to learn a hint of life's wisdom, my boy. If—"

"Oh, my!" Serenity's cry froze Timothy with his glass partway to his lips.

He did not hesitate as she gasped again. Shoving his glass into his grandfather's hand, he leaped across the room in a pair of steps. "What is wrong?"

Serenity continued to stare at Theodora, but whispered, "She moved it."

"It?"

Grasping Theodora's hand, Serenity blinked back tears of joy. Had she been mistaken? No, she was sure of what she had seen.

"You moved your arm!" she whispered.

Theodora stared at her right arm. "I did. It moved."

"Impossible!" The earl came to his feet and walked over to them, disbelief mixing with hope on his face. "We were told she would never be able to move it."

"Look for yourself." Serenity motioned to Theodora. "Can you do it again?"

The little girl wrinkled her face with concentration. Serenity stood and clenched her hands at her side. When Timothy took one in his, she did not look at him. His fingers were as rigid as hers as they waited to see if Theodora could shift her arm once more.

Theodora's elbow contracted so slightly that Serenity won-dered if she would have noticed if she had not been watching.

"I did it!" cried the little girl.

"You did!" Serenity hugged her. "She did it!"

She stepped back as the earl, unabashedly weeping, put his arms around Theodora. The little girl giggled and looked back at her right elbow. She strained to move it again.

Serenity cheered, then gasped as Timothy whirled her into his arms, embracing her as she had Theodora. When she started to ease out of his arms so she could congratulate the little girl, his arms tightened. She was tugged up against his chest. She looked up at him, startled. Before she could halt it, her hand brushed his face, and he grinned as broadly as Theodora.

"Shall we celebrate with Theodora now?" he asked quietly.

"Yes, certainly."

His voice dropped to a raw whisper. "And later alone?"

"Yes, certainly," she answered again, but with a quiver of anticipation that she could not submerge. It lingered, growing stronger each time Timothy's gaze met hers, while the earl ordered tea and cakes brought to toast Theodora's accomplishment.

"I must finish that device to assist her," Timothy said as Serenity walked with him toward the front of the house after both Theodora and the earl had retired for a nap.

"She will need it even more if she can continue to move her elbow. It is only a beginning, I realize, but if she continues to use it, she may find it easier and easier."

He slipped his arm around her waist while they walked past rooms draped in twilight as the early winter night claimed the moor. "As I find touching you?"

"It is hardly the same thing."

"Then mayhap I should have said *not* touching you."

She paused, baffled. She had been so sure that he shared her delight with the stolen caresses. "That is easier?"

"*Au contraire.* It is easier not to resist touching you."

She leaned her head against his shoulder, for she could no longer resist being close to him. There were not many days left until the earl's birthday celebration. Then . . . She did not know what she would do then, but the chance to savor him against her would be lost.

Timothy smiled as he stopped in front of a set of double doors that were intricately carved. She had passed them before and wondered what was on the other side.

As if he were privy to her thoughts again, he said, "I have noted how you glance at these doors each time you walk by them. Let me ease your curiosity, and tell you that here is where the ball will be held."

When he threw open the doors, she knew he had done it for the best effect. Windows that reached to the ceiling, which must be twice as high as the one here in the hall, were not softened by drapes. The half-moons at the top of each one welcomed in the thin winter moonlight to let it inch along the stone floor. In the very center of the floor, a fire pit suggested that this section of the house was almost as ancient as the moors themselves.

Serenity started to walk in, but stopped when Timothy took her hand. He picked up a lamp from a nearby table and smiled as he said, "The corners are dark. I am sure you want to explore each one."

"You know me well."

He squeezed her hand. "Not as well as I would like."

Slapping his arm lightly, she said, "You are a rogue, Timothy Crawford."

"I like the sound of that."

"Being a rogue?"

He laughed. "Just the way you say 'rogue' in such a teasing, admiring tone."

"I do admire the way you have chosen the life you want, rather than the one the Polite World would think should be yours." She started to add more, but simply stared as he held up the lamp to reveal gilt cherubs decorating the ceiling.

The golden paint outlined the intricate diamond pattern along the frescoes and walls. Each window glowed with the color running along the edges of the glass, as if sunlight had been captured within it. Flowers burst from vines of gold.

"This is like being in King Midas's garden," Serenity whispered.

He chuckled. "Just what I used to imagine when I could sneak in here as a child while it was being rebuilt."

"Was there a fire?"

"Yes. Only the stones of the fire pit in the center and the floor itself survived." He laughed again. "I was so pleased that Grandfather did not rebuild it to be a dreary medieval behemoth, as it had been."

She turned slowly to see as much as the lamplight allowed. "It's magical." She smiled. "This whole afternoon has been magical."

"Thanks to you."

"'Twas Theodora who—"

"'Twas *you*. You gave her the chance to try. None of us thought she could achieve anything but dying young."

"Timothy!"

"It is the truth, even though it is shameful to own to it. You have shown all of us—including Theodora—that we were wrong."

Serenity paused by one of the arched windows, and Timothy did, too. She started to speak, faltered, then blurted, "Will you promise me something?"

"Whatever you wish."

Whatever she wished? Did he truly want to hear how she wished this charade would go on forever, that she would be his beloved fiancée and mayhap one day his wife? Or would he really like to hear her say that she understood his obsession with building and inventing and solving problems that had betrayed him into making up the story of this betrothal?

She dampened her lips and watched his gaze follow the motion. Mayhap he would not be averse to the truth of what she wished, but she knew, as she lowered her eyes, that she could not speak it.

Instead she asked, "Will you promise me that you will take Theodora out to the pond this summer to see the ducklings?"

"Ducklings?" He shook himself as if he had been lost in a dream.

They both had—a dream of letting the lies become the truth—but nothing had changed. His grandfather was an earl, and hers was a forgotten memory.

"She has seen them only through the window," Serenity said with a weak smile. "I know she would love to sit on the grass on a sunny afternoon and watch them."

"I promise, Serenity, if you will make me a promise." He set the lamp on a bench by the wall.

"Whatever you wish."

Her hope that his eyes would twinkle mischievously vanished when his face remained somber. "Promise me that you will be here to join us by the pond."

"I wish I could."

"Serenity, you helped make the impossible happen this afternoon." He put his hands on her shoulders and let his fingers trickle along her arms like a healing rain. "How simple in comparison it would be to give us a look-in."

"Your life is your own, Timothy. You may come and go as you please. You may work or play as you please. I have no idea what my life is. Who knows? I may be scheduled to sail to India this spring." She tried to smile, but failed.

"You could stay here."

"Here?"

He nodded. "Why not? You are no closer to remembering where you belong than you were when you awoke at the inn. You have nowhere to go and every reason to stay."

"Save two."

"Your brother and sister?"

She sighed. "I must think of them."

"Will you think of *me* after you leave?"

"How can you ask that?"

"How can you leave?"

Serenity turned away to continue to the very edge of the circle of light. "Timothy, I thought you would understand better than anyone that my brother and sister are an obligation I cannot put aside. I should not want to put it aside."

His footfalls were quiet as he came to stand behind her. His hands swept down her arms, wrapping them around her with his arms over hers. When she rested her head back against him, she closed her eyes, thrilled to be surrounded by his tender strength.

"I do understand," he whispered.

She shivered as his breath stirred her hair and caressed her ear. It sent fire pulsing to the very tips of her toes.

"I just want you to stay here," he continued, "until you know more about what you have lost. I don't want you to feel obligated to leave with Twelfth Night."

"But if I stay . . ."

"The lie continues." He sighed and released her. As she turned, he caught her face between his broad hands. "But this also continues, sweetheart."

His lips brushed her with a gentleness that threatened to undo her completely. Putting her hands over his as he lifted his mouth away, she steered it back to hers. That one brief, captivating touch had not been enough.

With a hushed laugh, he pulled her up against him. The gentleness vanished as he captured her lips, kissing her with a deep, urgent need. His ragged sigh of pleasure stirred the fires deep in her soul in the moment before his lips etched sparks of pleasure across her cheeks. This was what she wanted, what she wanted him to promise her a lifetime of, what—

Serenity pulled out of Timothy's arms as she heard footsteps. Had she gone queer in the attic to surrender to her craving this way? *Sweet heavens!* No matter what Timothy offered, she had no future here. She had no future anywhere until she found her past.

"Over here!" Timothy called, startling her. Was he so eager to put this mistake behind him? When he looked at her with his eyes still glazed with pleasure, she knew what he truly was eager for.

As she was.

Serenity managed a strained smile as Felix and Melanda entered. When Felix shut the door behind them, she frowned. What was he about now?

With Melanda's hand on his arm, Felix led her across the long ballroom toward the lamplight. Their smiles looked much more sincere than her own, especially when they shared furtive glances.

"Are you giving Serenity the tuppence tour of the house?" Felix asked.

"The what?" Serenity returned.

Timothy smiled. "He means a quick tour." Looking at the others, he said, "I thought 'twas time she saw where we shall celebrate Grandfather's birthday on Christmas Eve." He laughed. "It is about time she saw it, because, as my betrothed, she shall be the hostess to our guests."

Excitement pulsed in Serenity at the thought of welcoming guests to this magnificent ballroom when it was decorated with greenery and candles and music. Around her would be glittering ladies and their elegant escorts . . . and Timothy. A thrill surged through her like a storm wave throwing itself up onto the shore. She would be at his side where she could relish his smiles and how his hand brushed hers. But that was no longer enough. She wanted to be swept again into his arms as he trailed kisses across her face.

Melanda laughed, her voice echoing off the high ceiling. "This will be wondrously grand. I wish the duchess could see this. She has bragged that her house has the biggest ballroom in all of England. It could easily fit within this room with space to spare."

"Cheyney Park is one of the hidden secrets of northern England." Felix smiled as if he had designed the house himself.

"If I were the chatelaine of this house, I would have assemblies here as often as possible." She turned to Serenity. "Don't you agree?"

Serenity smiled back. Clearly Felix had told Melanda about this charade, proving Timothy right that his cousin could not keep a secret. She wondered how Felix had halted himself from revealing the truth to the earl . . . and why.

"I like the quiet in here, too," Serenity said as she ran her fingers along the raised wood that made a diamond pattern crisscrossing the wall.

"I guess that is why you are called Serenity," Melanda said, her voice again sharp, as it usually was when she addressed anyone but Felix. "Too much quiet starts sounding far too loud."

Timothy chuckled under his breath as Melanda and Felix walked away to look at the fire pit. "They are two of a kind."

"Not happy unless they are enjoying the entertainments of Town?" Serenity asked.

"Exactly." He leaned back against a tall stone stand that she guessed would hold a plant or a statue during a party. "Grandfather should be grateful that they tore themselves away from Town long enough to come here."

"But there is so little to do in Town during the holiday season."

His eyes narrowed. "You say that with true authority, Serenity."

"I wish," she said, wrapping her arms around herself, "that I could claim it was a fragment of memory coming to the surface, but it seems that it would be something anyone might know."

"You are probably right. How do you endure not remembering your past?"

"I do not endure it easily."

"I should think not. I honestly thought you would have recalled the whole of it by now."

She closed her eyes and sighed. "I had hoped that I would. Now I wonder if it ever will return completely."

When he did not answer, she discovered him staring at the far side of the ballroom, as if he expected to discover all the answers imprinted on the wall.

"Timothy?" she whispered.

His gaze moved to her, and she saw regret in his eyes. Regret? For what?

"'Tis not your doing," she said quietly.

"Mayhap I should have heeded my instincts rather than Felix's idea. If I had arranged for you to be in a familiar place, you may have regained your memories with more alacrity."

She put her hand on his sleeve. "But what place would have been familiar? The inn was not." As her fingers glided along his arm, the flashes of heat returned to glow in his eyes. "Leaving me there would not have helped."

He grazed her cheek with the back of his hand. "Nor would we have had this opportunity to become acquainted." His voice softened. "Serenity . . ."

Holding her breath, she gazed up at him. The hunger in his voice burned in his eyes and deep within her. The sample of ecstasy in their interrupted kiss honed the desire for another, this one continuing until they were sated. But would a single kiss ever be sufficient when she was utterly addicted to this pleasure?

Melanda's laugh trilled around the room again. Serenity looked hastily away from Timothy's enthralling expression.

Bending, he picked up the lamp and gave her a wry grin. "Shall we find out what is so amusing?"

"Yes," she said, even though she yearned for this interlude to linger, holding them together for another pair of heartbeats.

Felix threw out his hands to emphasize a point and struck Timothy's arm. Serenity gasped as the lamp flew out of his fingers. No one moved when it shattered against the fire pit, the light vanishing to leave them in a blanket of darkness. Melanda's shriek hurt Serenity's ears.

Quietly Timothy said, "No need for alarm, Melanda. Allow your eyes to adjust, and the moonlight will be enough to guide you to the door. You should have left the door ajar, Felix."

"I thought some privacy would be nice," he grumbled.

Serenity bit her lip to keep from laughing as she heard Melanda's sharp intake of breath. Mayhap Felix and Melanda had not intended to intrude on her and Timothy. Mayhap, instead, they had been seeking a private place for a rendezvous. She could not forget how Theodora had spoken of seeing them kissing by the duck pond.

"*I* think we should take our leave while the moonlight remains," Timothy said. "With its help, we should have no difficulty reaching the door."

In spite of Timothy's reassuring words, he grasped Serenity's hand as they edged around the fire pit. She glanced at him and saw the faint sparkle of his smile in the dim light. For a moment she thought he was simply amused by his cousin and Melanda. Then, as he laced his fingers through hers, she saw that muted sparkle widen. She knew the truth. He had been as beguiled by their kiss as she was.

Fearful that everyone else could hear the sudden thunder of her heart, she held that thought close to cherish it. She was glad to think neither of the past nor the future, but to enjoy this moment when his thumb's clandestine caress against her palm sent bolts of delight through her.

Timothy opened the door and said, "I shall get someone to clean up the broken glass." He hurried along the hall.

Felix mumbled something before turning to Melanda, who sank to a nearby chair, her face as gray as if she had already succumbed to the vapors. When Melanda began to lament, Serenity wondered how she could be so distressed about something so incidental. Nobody had been hurt, save for the lamp.

Serenity wanted to take her leave as well, but she was unsure if Felix, who was wringing his hands as if he held a dishrag, would be able to help Melanda if she was consumed by a *crise de nerfs*. Glancing wistfully in the direction Timothy had chosen, she stood in silence and listened to Melanda bemoaning how she suffered through the darkness and how she would prefer to be anywhere but these desolate moors. Serenity was not quite certain what the moors had to do with a broken lamp and a shadowed ballroom, so she started to ease away. Melanda's voice was growing stronger and sharper with every complaint.

Just as she was about to excuse herself, Serenity froze. She gasped, "Are you talking about the Frost Fair several years ago in London? Did you attend, too?"

Felix's eyes slitted in that expression she was seeing too often lately when she mentioned anything about her past. "Too, Serenity? Are you recalling some more of what you have forgotten?"

"Just images." She frowned. "When someone mentions a word, I occasionally remember something. Nothing specific. Just something. When you said Frost Fair I was transported to the past for only a second. In that second I saw the colorful pavilions on the Thames, the crowds, and little else."

He shrugged. "That is of little use to you in remembering who you really are. Mayhap you have a reason for not wanting to remember the truth."

"Or mayhap she has recalled it," Melanda said with an abruptly gleeful smile. "She simply does not wish to own to that."

"If," Serenity replied in her coldest voice, "I am fortunate to remember anything of import, you may be assured that I shall announce it from the highest roof of Cheyney Park so that no one will fail to heed it."

"Save Grandfather." Felix's laugh again had a brittle edge. "You would be wise to remember that you agreed to keep that knowledge to yourself until after Grandfather's party."

"If you will recall, we all agreed to keep our counsel about this." She glanced at Melanda.

Felix's face turned an unhealthy crimson. Jerking Melanda to her feet, he steered her along the passage in the direction opposite the one Timothy had chosen.

Serenity watched them walk away. Felix was distressed. How much more distressed would he be if she told him how she grew more certain with the passage of each day that she had met him and his father before? But where? Under what circumstances? She could not accuse him of keeping the truth of that meeting from her when he had been unable to keep from divulging the truth of her masquerade to both his father and Melanda.

But he has kept the secret from his grandfather!

She wished that thought had remained silent. In the weeks she had been at Cheyney Park, she had come to know this family so much better. Yet Felix Wayne seemed even more a stranger than ever. His bonhomie covered emotions that she hesitated to confront.

She wondered what would happen if she did.

TWELVE

*T*he wind swirled around Serenity, plucking at her bonnet and scouring her face. Sunshine was eye-wrenchingly bright on the snow. Pulling her bonnet forward, she squinted past the hedges that tried to civilize this garden that had been stolen from the gorse and grasses of the moor.

She tried to envision this garden when spring bedecked it with flowers. It was impossible, because her spirits were too mired to let her imagination soar. By this week's end, she would be looking at leaving Cheyney Park, and she had no idea where she should go.

You can stay here.

The memory of Timothy's words and the hope in his eyes when he spoke them were seared in her brain. Not even a carriage accident could erase those memories. Mayhap because they were truly not in her brain, but in her heart.

She put her hand over the buttons on her dark blue coat. He could not be the first one in her heart, for she had had a family. A mother who had died, a father who might be alive or dead, and a sister and a brother who were as unseen as the notes of a song. These people must have a place in her heart, if only she could figure out a way to find them.

When the snow crunched behind her, Serenity looked over her shoulder. She smiled as her heart leaped at the sight of Timothy striding toward her. His dark cloak flapped behind him as if it were trying to fly away from the wintry day. Beneath it, his buckskin breeches and dark coat were molded to his strong body by the wind. He must have given up any attempt to keep on a hat, because his tawny hair swirled into his eyes.

"What are you doing out here in the cold?" Serenity asked as he came up to her.

"I was checking with the stables about the final details for arrangements for the horses and carriages of Grandfather's guests. I saw you walking out here." He grinned as the wind slammed into them, knocking her against him. "What are *you* doing out here in the cold?"

"I like these wintry days."

"I think I am beginning to." He chuckled as he put his arm around her and squeezed her shoulders. "I could get very fond of this wind."

"'Tis not just the wind." She smiled. She stepped away and turned to admire the gardens. "With the fresh snow, everything looks brand-new. To everyone, not just to me."

When he offered his arm, she put hers through it. He led her toward the water garden. Although she wondered what he expected to find there, save for the reeds that were frozen into the ice, she matched her steps to his. She wanted to enjoy every moment of the few they had left to share.

"You are constantly amazing me with your comments, Serenity," he said, as he helped her down some stone steps that were edged with ice.

"How?"

"I don't know if I could be as accepting of losing all my memories as you are."

"You have said that before, and I have told you that I am not accepting of it. Not in the least." She laughed. "I have considered asking everyone for the same gift this holiday—the truth about what happened to me before that carriage accident."

"I wish I could tell you."

"You have heard nothing from London?" She paused to face him. The wind threw his cloak around her, so they were alone within its ebony shadow.

His smile vanished. "Nothing that will help you."

She put her hands on his coatsleeves. "What is it, Timothy?"

"Nothing to distress you. A setback with the start of the next factory."

"I am so sorry."

He stared at her, bafflement lining his face. "You are, are you not?"

"I know how important these projects are to you. You revel in the challenges and the escape they give you from the *ton*."

"I guess it is pretty obvious."

It is to the woman who loves you.

Serenity edged away from him and continued down another set of steps. *Sweet heavens!* Where had that thought come from? She could not be falling in love with Timothy. He was the heir to an earl, and she was . . . She was no closer to knowing what she was than she had been the day she arrived at Cheyney Park.

"I did not mean to bore you with this discussion," Timothy said, taking the steps two at a time to catch up with her.

"It was not boring me."

"Then why are you running off?"

She forced a smile. It must have looked sincere, because he smiled back as she said, "If you have not noticed, my lord, it is downright cold. Standing still reminds me exactly how deeply the wind bites."

"I don't need a reminder of that." He put his arm around her shoulders. "This is just to keep warm."

"Really?" she asked when his eyes twinkled like the sunlight on the pond's ice.

"Yes, really, although it is an excellent excuse to stand close to you."

"You are being outrageous today." She hesitated, then asked, "Do you always do that when you don't want anyone to see that you are distressed?"

"Always."

"Then why has not anyone else figured out that you are distressed?"

He squeezed her shoulders as he had before. "Because they are caught up in all the plans for the holidays. Mrs. Gray told me yesterday morning that the cake for Grandfather's birthday will be four layers high."

"Five." She laughed. "She decided yesterday *afternoon* that four was not grand enough."

"Thank goodness she has not considered making it seven layers high, one for each decade."

"The cake is not done yet."

Timothy chuckled as they continued down the steps. She let the sound of his good humor surround her with a warmth that not even her cloak could match. While they walked through the winter garden, he pointed out where the flower beds would offer glorious color in just a few months. She slowly began to see the pattern of beauty that would be a joy for the eyes.

As they came around a corner of the curtain wall that extended into the garden, Serenity stared at a building that looked like no other building she had seen at Cheyney Park. Its roof arched up at the eaves, and it was hung with the tatters of paper lanterns that bounced mournfully in the wind.

"It is a Chinese building!" She peered closer at the carving on the walls. "Or it is supposed to be a Chinese building."

"Exactly right." He ducked his head to go through the low door beneath the odd roof.

When she followed, she found the room inside empty, save for benches ringing the edges. The weak sunlight poured down through clerestory windows that must be hidden in the roof, so no one outside the building could see them. Her fingers found carvings on the walls, but it was too shadowed to see what it was.

"A dragon over there," Timothy said, smiling, before she could ask. "I think there is a tree of some sort over here. Or mayhap this is the wall with a mountain and a river on it. I don't remember which is which."

"Your grandfather is fond of things of the Far East, is he not?"

"Actually it was my father who was." He sat on one of the stone benches, then stood with a grimace. "Dashed cold!"

Crossing her arms in front of her and slipping her hands under her arms, she mused, "So your father had this built? Did he travel to the East?" This place seemed oddly familiar, even though she could not guess why. It was the same sensation as when she had seen the temple lions . . . and Felix and his father. She could not guess how they all had been connected.

"No, I don't believe he had a chance to travel there." He touched one of the carvings. "Grandfather told me only that my father was deeply intrigued with things of the East since the time he went to Oxford. One of his friends who had actually been to the East helped him design this building. It is one of the few connections I have with my father, because he died so young. The portrait of him as a young man burned when the ballroom did, so I have only pictures of him as a young child at Grandfather's knee."

Sorrow thickened her throat. "Have you thought of contacting his friend who helped him with this building?"

"I had considered it, but Sir Philip is often traveling and seldom at his estate near the coast. Mayhap one of these days I shall think of it at a time when he is in residence there."

She put her hand on his arm. "You could write him a note. If he was your father's tie-mate, surely he would be eager to see how his friend's son has turned out. Mayhap there are other connections you have with your father than this building."

"You are ever an optimist, Serenity." He smiled as his fingers covered hers on his sleeve.

"I have to be."

Drawing her back out into the sunshine, he took a deep breath of the fresh air. "And I think you are right. I shall send Sir Philip a note at Loughlin Hall. He might receive us during the holidays, if he is there."

"Loughlin Hall?" She froze as if the wind had turned her to ice.

"Does it mean something to you?" He caught her by the shoulders and spun her to face him.

"I thought . . ." She sighed and shook her head. "For a moment there seemed to be something, but it is gone. Loughlin Hall. Loughlin Hall. Loughlin Hall."

"You cannot force it, Serenity."

"Being patient and waiting for my memory to return has not worked." Her hands curled into fists. "I hate this. I hate it so much!"

His arms enfolded her to him. "I know, sweetheart."

She closed her eyes and listened to his heartbeat. It became swift when her arms glided beneath his cloak to curve up along his back. Although she wanted to remain like this, never moving, she swallowed her sigh when he shivered and stepped back to draw her hand within his arm, so they could return to the house. She could not forget the dangerous wind or the peril of being so close to him when her heart was so wide open. How easy it would be to tell him that she appreciated his compassion, that she thrilled at his touch, that she loved him!

"Look. A duck's nest among the reeds." Timothy's voice jolted her out of her reverie that could lead only to more complications. "This must be the home of Theodora's ducklings."

Hoping her voice would not betray her thoughts, she asked, "You miss being here in the country, don't you?"

He nodded. "Very much. London has its entertainments, but anything that grows there must be restrained to remain within its boundaries. The flowers that bloom in Green Park would never be allowed to join those near Buckingham Palace. Each bed is a separate island." Standing and wiping his gloved hands on his breeches, he scanned the gardens. "Here there is a flow of one garden to another. And beyond the walls, the moors prove that true beauty cannot be contained by man."

"I love walking along the hills in the springtime when the gorse is just coming awake again from its winter slumber. The sheep are wandering free, and the birds dart to and fro, looking for materials for their nests and the babes that soon will come. It is best at dawn, when anything seems possible, and the day promises everything. As if . . ." She looked up at him. "Why can I see that so clearly when so much of my past is lost in shadows?"

"At least you know you are not that far from home."

"These moors are expansive. I could have started my walk upon them from dozens of directions." She tucked her mittened hands under her crossed arms and walked back toward the steps leading to the upper garden.

"Serenity?"

She looked back over her shoulder. "I know you were trying to make me feel better, but a taste of the truth seems like a torment instead of a relief."

"I don't want you to be tormented. If there was anything I could do, you know I would."

"I know."

"Even if it meant your leaving Cheyney Park right now."

But I do not want to go right now. Again she was glad those words had been in her head, not on her lips. She could not imagine a day without Timothy in it. Nor could she imagine being without his laugh, his kindnesses, his eyes that bespoke the yearning that taunted her as well.

"I promised you that I would stay to see this through, no matter what," she said.

"I appreciate that, Serenity, but I have been thinking lately about those who must be missing you."

She was glad when he put his arm around her again, because the ice within her was even more frigid than the wintry wind. "I have thought of that often. I wonder how I would fare if someone I cared for vanished without a trace. It is not just me, but the others who were traveling with me."

"They have not been identified either. If there was anything in the carriage to offer a clue, it was stolen before we were able to look for it."

"I appreciate that you have tried."

"Don't give up yet." He turned her to face him. "I have not."

Timothy fought to draw a breath as he gazed down into her eyes that glistened with unshed tears. No one had ever had more right to surrender to vapors than Serenity Adams did. In spite of that, she remained as strong as the walls of Cheyney Park.

He curved his hands along her face. He did not need to hear Felix's irritating voice urging him to take full advantage of this situation. Every inch of him was repeating it. This was the woman he had devised out of his dreams. Only a widgeon would let her walk out of his life without giving her a few memories to replace the ones she had lost.

With a silent groan, he turned away. She had done all he asked, providing him with a way to hide his shameful lies. He could not compound that shame by seducing her.

He had not turned away quickly enough, for he had caught a glimpse of her shock that he had not kissed her. *Dash it!* Did she have any idea how difficult this was for him? He had been a fool to taste those beguiling lips even once.

Not saying anything, he hurried her toward the house. There were not many more days before Grandfather's birthday celebration, and then . . .

And then what? Would he send Serenity on her way? Impossible, even if she had a place to go. Having her stay here after he left would be foolish, because every passing hour threatened the truth becoming known, and she should not face that moment alone, when the lie was his. He could bring her to Town, but, whether he set her up in her own house or as a guest in his, the gossipmongers of the *ton* would label her his high-flyer. That would ruin her reputation, and, if she truly was an abigail, no household would ever hire her again.

He must think of a solution. If she were to regain her memories . . . No, he could not depend on that, although he wished that for her.

Branson was waiting to hold the door as the wind herded them into the foyer. From the railing overlooking the foyer, Theodora waved as her nurse carried her toward the earl's sitting room.

When Serenity scurried back out the door, Timothy exchanged a baffled frown with the butler. What was she up to now? He never was quite sure with Serenity. Unlike everything else in his life that could be put in order with a minimum of fuss, she created this charming uproar.

She ran back into the house and up the stairs. Curiosity spurred his feet to follow. With a laugh, he paused in the doorway to his grandfather's sitting room. Theodora was perched in her favorite chair again, and Serenity was kneeling beside her as she placed a snowball in the little girl's hand.

"It is so cold!" Theodora gasped.

"Not as cold as the wind." Serenity shrugged off her coat and let it fall behind her on the carpet.

Timothy picked it up and settled it over his arm as he watched the little girl stare at the snow as if she had never seen it this close. With a flinch, he suspected she probably had not. How many more ways was Serenity gently going to remind them of how a tender heart could be a greater cure than all the advice of all the doctors in England?

"Next time we will take you with us. Right, Timothy?" Before he could answer, she went on, "You do have a coat, don't you?"

"You would have to ask Nurse," Theodora said.

"I shall." She wiped the melting snow from Theodora's hand and stood. Smiling at Timothy, she slipped her hand into his. "We shall have fun together outside."

"You can kiss Timothy, you know, like Felix and Melanda did." Theodora lowered her voice. "I will not look if you do not want me to."

Timothy laughed, unable to halt himself. Theodora was as serious as an old tough, urging her charge to flirt with a highly eligible bachelor.

"All you need to worry about when you go down to the pond with us is finding the ducklings' nest," he said.

Her eyes grew round. "Do you think ducks kiss, too?"

"I don't know. Have you ever seen them kiss?" She shook her head. "All they do is waddle about, and when Nurse opens the window I can hear them quacking. I so would like to touch one."

"We shall have to see about that, won't we, Serenity?" Serenity smiled. "Timothy has promised me that he will take you down to the pond to see the ducklings as soon as they hatch. Of course, the mother and father ducks may not want you to touch them right away, but you can see them up close."

"And will you come, too, Serenity?"

"I—"

"Timothy, thank heavens, you are here!" Melanda rushed into the room, her hair, for once, as tangled as if she had been out in the wind. Her colorless cheeks, however, warned that she had not suffered from the wind's fierce caress.

He caught her before she could fly right past him, so lost was she in her despair. "What is it, Melanda?"

"'Tis Felix."

"What about Felix?" He glanced at Serenity and saw his disquiet mirrored on her face. If Felix and Melanda had had a brangle, discussing it in front of Theodora was a mistaken thing. He wished he could ask Melanda to step out into the hallway, but that would create more questions from the little girl who was watching, wide-eyed.

"He is missing!" Melanda swayed.

Timothy caught her before she could fall. Settling her back on the settee, he heard Serenity say she would ring for *sal volatile*.

A throat was cleared nearer the door. "My lord?"

Coming to his feet as Serenity bent over Melanda and began to chafe the senseless woman's wrists, Timothy asked, "Branson, do you know anything of this?"

"Only what Miss Hayes said, my lord. It seems that Mister Felix is missing."

"Felix is missing? How did she decide that?" He had not guessed that his cousin would bestir himself from the chair closest to the hearth.

"Miss Hayes did not say, my lord, but she is clearly beyond distressed."

"My uncle—"

"Is not in, my lord. He has gone to call on a friend on the other side of the village."

Timothy groaned. "Has Felix taken leave of all sense? All right. Let's do a search of the outbuildings and the gardens. If he is not found, we shall look farther afield."

"Very good, my lord." Branson hurried out to make the arrangements.

Turning back to Serenity, Timothy said, "Stay here with Theodora, if you will."

"Gladly." Serenity gave the little girl a bolstering smile, then offered the same to him. He appreciated it more than he could ever voice.

His fingers caressed her soft cheek. "Both of you please keep an eye on Grandfather. Melanda will just upset him with her vapors. Uncle Arnold is not much better in a crisis, so be prepared if he returns."

"I will."

He put his hands on her shoulders and drew her to her feet and away from Theodora, who was listening avidly. "Keep Melanda and my uncle away from Grandfather. Please."

"I shall do my best."

"I know you will. Thank you." He bent toward her.

This time he could not resist the lure of her wine red lips. Her soft gasp warned of her surprise that he would kiss her when Theodora was watching. The sound vanished beneath his mouth as his arms enveloped her, pulling her up against his chest.

With a groan of his own, he released her and rushed out of the room while he still could. His cousin might be in trouble, but he could think only of Serenity and what they could share when he returned.

THIRTEEN

$\mathcal{E}$gad!"

Serenity paused by the top of the stairs to look down at the foyer. Timothy was standing in the very middle, scowling at an evergreen tree that was dripping melting snow onto the stones. "Welcome home!" she called.

Before she could ask if he had found his cousin, Timothy asked, "Why is there a blasted tree in the foyer?" He shrugged off his coat and walked around the tree that had its branches still intact. If it had been stood on its cut base, it would have been no taller than he was. "If that is to be our Yule log, it is sadly lacking in breadth as well as height."

Serenity folded her arms on the upper banister. "You should ask your Aunt Ilse. She had one of the stablemen bring it in not more than five minutes ago. Did you find Felix? What happened to him?"

He smiled. "Aunt Ilse, is it? Who knows what she may have in mind? She has been as excited as any of the children with the advent of Christmas. Where is she?"

"She mumbled something about wondering if there would be enough small candles in the storeroom, then hurried off toward the kitchen." Serenity came down the stairs and stepped over a puddle where snow had fallen off the fir branches. "She asked me to gather up any children in the household so they could help."

"Help with what?"

She shook her head. "I have no idea. Mayhap she wants to allow them to have a small Yule log of their own."

"I hope she does not plan to burn it in the parlor's fireplace. It would create a fearsome mess in there."

"Timothy! What about Felix?"

He grimaced. "He is fine. I shall tell you all about it when there are fewer ears about." He tugged on one of the branches, and needles scattered onto the floor. "These should have been cut off before it was brought into the house."

"She insisted that the branches be left on." Serenity tried to keep her voice cheerful, but was curious why Timothy wanted to hide what he had discovered about his cousin.

"Why does Aunt Ilse want the branches left on?"

"I have no idea. Mayhap it is something they do in her prince's household."

"She has picked up some strange habits as well as her name."

"Her name?" Serenity climbed back up the stairs with him.

"Her birth name is Elsbeth, but she changed it to Ilse when she married Rupert."

"So I am not the only one with a different name." She gasped, wanting to take back the words that might betray Timothy's plan.

As if nothing were amiss, he laughed. "Women are accustomed to changing their names when they marry, but usually not their given names, too. I think you should keep Serenity. Serenity Crawford." He paused as they reached the upper gallery. Taking her hand, he bowed over it. "My Lady Cheyney."

She knew she should say something jesting in return, but no words came into her head as he stood, his gaze capturing hers. How wondrous it sounded to be addressed so! She could not imagine how glorious it would be if she truly were his betrothed.

"My lord," she whispered, knowing she must say something.

But that was the wrong thing to say in the wrong tone, she realized, when the fires in his eyes swirled around her and within her in an invitation to be a part of that vivid flame. He said nothing while he drew her into a nearby room and shut the door.

She was in his arms, her mouth against his, before she had time to form a single thought. The day's cold sifted from his coat through the fine material of her gown, but all she knew was the sweet warmth of his kiss. When his mouth left hers to taste the line of her pulse along her neck, she gripped his arms, afraid that this rapture would consume her even as she wanted more. His lips brushed the curve of her breast above her modest gown, and she moaned with the need that would be silent no longer. He answered with the soft whisper of her name as his fingers combed up into her hair to pull her mouth to his again.

Serenity jerked herself away. Had she lost her mind? She was not Serenity Adams! She was not the fantasy that chance had brought to life for Timothy. Yet . . . Her fingers rose toward his face as he cupped her elbows. Mayhap she was more wantwitted not to take advantage of what might be her last chance to be in the arms of a man she loved.

She started to step toward him, but paused as a knock sounded at the door. It opened, and the earl peeked in like a naughty child.

"Am I interrupting something?" he asked.

Although Serenity had the peculiar feeling that he wanted her to say yes, she said, "Of course not. Do come in and join us."

"If you are sure I am not interrupting." He glanced at his grandson. Now she was certain the earl had hoped to intrude upon a private moment, that he wanted his heir and his heir's fiancée to be mad about one another.

Timothy drew off his gloves. "Grandfather, Serenity assured you that you were not."

"As long as you are *sure*?"

"Yes, of course." She took the old man's hand and led him to sit on the settee closest to the hearth. "I was just about to ask Timothy what news he had of Felix's present whereabouts."

"I see that you were." Lord Brookindale pushed a strand of her hair back from her face.

She realized that her hair was undone and hanging about her shoulders. When had that happened? Slipping the strand back behind her ear, she hoped her face was not as red as Timothy's, which had been scratched by the wind's claws.

The earl looked at his grandson with an abrupt frown. "Felix's whereabouts? Is the boy missing?" He sighed. "One would have guessed he had given up such childish habits along with his childhood."

Timothy shook his head as he held out his hands to warm them. "We thought he was missing, but I should have known better than to listen to Melanda's caterwauling."

"She seemed genuinely concerned," Serenity interjected, surprising herself as much as the men that she was defending Melanda.

"I suspect she was." Timothy smiled. "However, her concerns were misplaced. Felix has ridden over to his father's house to retrieve a cravat that Uncle Arnold left behind by mistake."

"All of this hubbub because of a cravat?" Serenity sat on the arm of a chair, glad for the excuse to give her wobbly knees a rest. She wondered why Timothy was so solicitous of his cousin. Clearly he had not wanted to damage Felix in the household's eyes. Yet Felix could be beastly to Timothy. To hide her disquieting thoughts, she said, "Really, sometimes I think the Polite World has no sense at all."

"Sometimes I think you are right."

"And the rest of the time?"

He turned and propped his chin on his thumb. "The rest of the time, I *know* you are right."

"So you agree that it would be jobbernowl not to have Theodora go outside with us on our next stroll." She smiled. For some things it was better to have extra ears listening. She needed any allies she could find for this discussion.

"What is this?" asked the earl.

Timothy's scowl returned. "Serenity wants to take Theodora outside to experience the snow and wind and cold for herself."

"No." The earl shook his head. "That is impossible. If the child were to take a chill, heaven alone knows what the effect would be."

"I would be certain," Serenity said, struggling to keep her smile in place, for she had hoped that the earl would see that this idea was inspired, "that Theodora is so bundled up that she could not move as much as her good arm. Mrs. Gray told me that there would be mumming plays in the village for the holiday. Every child should have a chance to see them."

Lord Brookindale's scowl was nearly identical to his grandson's. "Serenity, until this moment I had considered you a woman of rare good sense. It seems it has taken leave of you."

Coming to her feet, she said, "Theodora needs to experience everything any other child might experience. I know you fear for her health, but what good is it to keep her cosseted when who knows if this might be her last holiday? I know that sounds heartless—"

"No," said Timothy with a sigh, "it sounds quite the opposite. You are thinking with your heart, Serenity, allowing it to cloud your judgment."

"I have thought this through. If we take her in a closed carriage—"

Timothy shook his head. "The roads are treacherous at best, and the hill leading down into the village is steep. A carriage is dangerous under those conditions."

"I know." She did not lower her eyes, even though a pulse of pain lashed her. One memory she did not want to return was the memory of the accident that had left her not knowing who she was. Quietly she went on, "Then we shall take a sleigh. We can have hot stones to keep us warm as well as thick blankets. We will watch part of the performance and return before the stones grow cold." She knelt by the earl's chair. "Please let me do this for her. I fear that I will be unable to fulfill any other promises I have made to her."

She heard Timothy's muttered curse as he walked away to stand before the hearth again. Timothy understood what she could not say to his grandfather. It was not Theodora's health that would keep Serenity from doing as she had promised the little girl, but the ending of this interlude as Serenity Adams.

"Let me consider this," the earl said with a sigh.

Timothy said in a growl, "Grandfather—"

"I shall give you my answer at dinner this evening." He set himself on his feet. "Why don't you two go and enjoy the greening of the chapel while I give this some thought?"

Serenity clasped her hands behind her back after coming to her feet. As the earl walked out of the room, she waited for Timothy to speak again. No matter what she said now, it might be the wrong thing.

"There is no use in fooling ourselves, is there?" Timothy asked as he stepped away from the hearth. "The masquerade is nearly at its end."

"Masquerade?" asked Felix from the door.

Turning, Serenity was amazed to see that his face had nearly as little color as the snow in the garden. He lurched forward and put his hand on the back of the closest chair, as if he feared he would swoon as Melanda had.

"Is something wrong?" Timothy fired back. "Other than your causing a to-do in this house by letting Melanda think that you had vanished."

"She overreacts sometimes." He waved at his cousin weakly. "I told her I would be here in time to help with the greening of the chapel." He swallowed so roughly that Serenity heard it. "What is this about the masquerade being over?"

Timothy picked up his gloves and slapped them against his palm. "Did you take a knock in the skull while you were out riding? You know as well as we do what I spoke of. Serenity is needed here only until Grandfather's birthday celebration, which is only a few days from now."

"Oh, *that* masquerade."

"What other one could there be?" Serenity asked. Felix Wayne was one of the most vexing people she had met . . . or could recall meeting. As Melanda was the second most exasperating, they were two of a kind.

"You are right." He pushed himself to stand straighter. "I am just caught up in the skimble-skamble silliness of the holiday season."

Timothy picked up his coat and folded it over his arm. "Have you spoken with Melanda to set her mind at ease?"

"Her abigail assured me that she was resting comfortably, but would not be joining us for the greening of the chapel. Apparently she needs time to recover from her tears of despair at what she persuaded herself was the end of my existence."

He motioned toward the door. "Shall we?"

"As long as we do not have to tote Aunt Ilse's tree back to the chapel."

Timothy handed his coat and gloves to a maid. "Tree?"

Serenity looked over the rail at the same time Timothy did. The evergreen tree had vanished from the foyer, but a trail of needles warned that it had been brought up to this floor and into a room across the hall from the double doors to the ballroom.

Not waiting for the others, Serenity went to the door to see Aunt Ilse draping the tree, which had been set into a pot in front of the trio of windows, with the strands of dried fruit she and the others had strung. Aunt Ilse was humming some song that Serenity did not recognize. Even when Aunt Ilse began to sing, the words must have been in German, because Serenity could not understand any of them. A half dozen children were sitting on the floor, watching with smiles. In a chair right next to the tree, Theodora grinned like a satisfied cat.

"Are you coming to join us in decorating our *Tannenbaum*?" asked Aunt Ilse.

"*Tannenbaum*?"

"A Christmas tree!" Theodora crowed, and the other children giggled. "That is what this is, Serenity. A Christmas tree."

"But what is a Christmas tree?" Serenity asked.

Aunt Ilse did not halt in arranging the fruit strands on the branches, letting the strings droop like swags. "It is a tradition among the German states. Instead of bringing a tree in to burn it on the hearth, as is done in England with a Yule log, in my husband's country we bring a tree inside and decorate it with fruit and candles. Children, do you want to help?"

Serenity stepped back into the hall as the children ran to assist Aunt Ilse. She wondered if the tree would survive their ministrations.

"Very odd," she said, as she joined Timothy and Felix on the stairs.

"That is an apt description of Aunt Ilse." Felix's laugh was sharp. "She has assumed the ways of her adopted homeland as if she were a native."

"I would say that is wise of her. A princess should understand and respect her subjects and their traditions, no matter how curious they may be." Serenity smiled. "I suspect they quite adore her."

Timothy chuckled when he paused at the bottom of the stairs and offered his arm. As he drew her fingers into it and put his hand over hers, he said, "You are as insightful as always. Whenever Aunt Ilse visits England, she receives letters from her husband's countrymen and -women urging her to return home soon and safely. They miss her dearly when she is away."

"Or," Felix said in the same grumbling tone, "they are so driven to ennui by her boring husband that they are eager for her to come back and entertain them with her bizarre ways."

"I am sure," Serenity added quietly as if Felix had not spoken, "they adore her as much as the children here do. As much as you do, Timothy."

"Me?"

She laughed as they walked toward the oldest section of the house. "I have seen you sitting and chatting with her, and you are always smiling as broadly as the children do when she is about. You enjoy her as much as they do."

"As I said, you are insightful, sweetheart."

Serenity's smile at the endearment faltered when she saw Felix glower at his cousin. Was Felix being the most sensible of all of them to remember that this *was* truly a masquerade that would end with the ringing in of Christmas?

Her uneasiness grew when they came around a corner in the hall and discovered greens piled by the ancient door of what was clearly a chapel that had been built at least four hundred years before. The pews, which offered seating for no more than a score, were wooden and showed the stains of each passing year. A simple altar carved of the same stone as the walls was set at the front.

When Felix pushed past her to scoop up an armload, she realized Timothy was hesitating, too. Did Timothy share her disquiet at entering this chapel when they were lathered with lies?

He glanced at her and quickly away, but not before she saw the flush rising along his face. Had she seen embarrassment or anger that, by being here, she was ruining a tradition he loved? She put her hand on his arm again, and he squeezed her fingers before bending to collect some of the greens.

"Shall we?" His voice was strained.

"It seems that we should, as we are right here."

"It will be all right, Serenity," he said in a near whisper.

"I wish I could believe that. I am not sure of anything any longer."

"I am." He halted her from bending to gather up some greens. Ignoring the servants, who were carrying more armloads into the passage, he stroked her cheek. "I am sure that having you here is better than never having had the chance to know you."

"But you don't know *me*. I don't."

"Mayhap not." He brushed her cheek with a swift kiss. "But I cannot believe that the true part of you could be changed even by an accident."

Serenity did not know what to say, and she had no chance, even if she could have found the right words. The laughter and excitement of the decorating lured her into the chapel. Soon she put her dreary thoughts aside as she let the joy in the chapel seep into her. She laughed along with the others as they tried to clean sap from their fingers and ended up only making them dirtier. Hearing Timothy chuckle at some jest among the men who were hanging the greenery from the rafters overhead, she bent to help the women who were securing garlands of greenery to the pews and around the altar.

Because they did not have to climb up and down the ladders, the women's work was done more quickly. Serenity took a deep breath of the evergreens as she gathered up some of the pieces that had fallen from the strands now circling the chapel. She tossed the broken branches into a pile by the door, where they could be swept outside.

She started to turn to pick up more, then paused. The sounds of laughter and teasing seemed to vanish as she knelt to pull out two straight branches. She stared at them, wanting to believe that this fragment of memory was real and not just wishful thinking. Holding the branches, she rose and groped for the closest pew. She sat and continued to stare at them.

"What is so fascinating?" asked Timothy as he walked over to her.

Slowly she raised her eyes to meet the good humor in his. She watched them narrow as she whispered, "This could work for Theodora."

"Two sticks?" His laugh sounded forced. "Serenity, she cannot hold but one."

"No, look!" She broke the branches over her knee. Tossing aside the longer pieces, she held up two sticks. Each was about ten inches long. She balanced both of them in one hand, so she could wiggle them and bring the tips together. "If she used them like this . . ."

Timothy squatted beside her and reached for her hand. When she started to give him the sticks, he shook his head. "No, hold them as you were holding them. I want to watch you move them."

"Do you think this really could work for her?"

"I don't know yet. Let me see how you open and close the tips of the sticks."

Serenity slowly raised and lowered the top stick. "The bottom one stays pretty much stationary."

"Amazing! How did you come up with this idea?"

"I did not." She laughed and bent to pick up a piece of ivy up from the floor with the two sticks. "The Chinese invented these centuries ago. They use chopsticks for eating instead of a fork."

Timothy gripped her elbows as he rose far enough to sit beside her. "How do you know that? That is not something an abigail would know, is it?"

"No," she said slowly, "it is not." Gazing down at the sticks in her hand, she whispered, "My father told me about using chopsticks. I know he did. I can remember him teaching me to use them. We laughed a lot because I was so clumsy with them." She touched the other end of the sticks. "He lashed the upper end together for me, so I could use them like a crab's claws, pinching them together."

"Which would work perfectly for Theodora."

"Do you think you could make something like this?"

He chuckled. "You tell me that your father did it for you. I cannot resist the challenge of re-creating something that has already been created."

"And improving on it, because you will have to hook the sticks to the straps to go around her arm."

"That part is already designed, although I want to make the straps easy enough to use that she can put the device on and take it off by herself." He shook his head with a wry grin. "So simple. I was trying to make it far too complicated."

"I wish I had thought of this earlier."

His expression became somber. "You are remembering more and more. Have you recalled *anything* that will help us discover who you really are?"

"My father taught me about Eastern art and utensils. How many men can there be with that knowledge?"

"Any captain who has sailed to buy tea in China or any soldier who has been to the East or any gentleman who might be intrigued with the study of the East, as my father was."

She sighed. "Your point is well-taken. I guess it does not help."

"But it does." He tapped her cheek with his fingertip. "There are many men who have no interest in the East. All we must do is look for one who does and who can tell us the truth of your past."

"What if he is dead?" She could barely voice the fear that had taunted her since the first memories began to assert themselves. "If I am the sole caretaker of my sister and brother, then both of our parents must be dead."

"You cannot be certain you have understood that single letter correctly. If you handled your father's accounts, it would be your duty to send the money for your siblings' schooling."

"An abigail would not be involved in such things, would she?"

"I am not assuming anything about your past any longer." He stood and held out his hand. "Let us get the rest of this greenery strung around the chapel. I am anxious to get back to work on making Theodora's page-turner."

She looked around as she stood. "It seems as if the work is completed."

"So there is no need for this length of greenery." His eyes took on that mischievous twinkle that she adored. "Or is there?"

He looped the run of greens around her. His eyes glittered more brightly than the candles as he stepped nearer. She needed only to edge back, and the greens would shatter, releasing her. She would be free. Free of the verdant bonds, but not free from the longing to stand like this . . . and closer.

His hands rose, and the backs of his fingers brushed her cheek. She closed her eyes, delighting in the pleasure that she could not believe she once had feared she would have to feign. When had the game become reality? When had the lie evolved into the truth?

The others' voices faded once more until she was certain she could hear Timothy's heartbeat along with her own. When his hand glided along her skin to cup her chin, he tipped her face toward his. In the second before his lips covered hers, he murmured, "You set my soul on fire with your sweet touch. I want you to quench it with your kisses."

Her answer was silenced by the demand of his lips. As she put her arms around his shoulders, she wondered if she could continue to resist the desires neither of them would be able to control much longer. It was a question she did not think of. At that moment, as he thrilled her with his mouth's fevered caress, she forgot everything but this pleasure she had yearned to sample.

When his tongue delved past her lips and into the hidden delights, she clutched his shoulders, unable to move, unable to think as she struggled against the engulfing tide of rapture. Nothing had warned her of the power of this sorcery that stripped her of all thought.

He released her, and she sagged against him, her breath as uneven as the rapid beat of her heart. When he again put a single fingertip under her chin to tilt her mouth beneath his, she answered his yearning with her own.

Mayhap she was a fool, but she would be one for as long as she could, because, although her heart had changed and now yearned to belong to him, one thing had not changed.

She was not Serenity Adams. When Christmas dawned, this fairy tale of falling in love with the man of her dreams would come to an end.

FOURTEEN

$\mathcal{A}$re you ready to leave?"

Timothy looked up from the accounts book that he should have checked two days ago. Odd how when Serenity was about he was not the least interested in the family's enterprises. He had not been able to put the factories and their output from his mind even when he had been sitting with Charlene. It was quite the opposite with Serenity. She did not even need to be in the room for his thoughts to be focused on her beguiling smile or the way her eyes burned with silver fire when she could not govern her emotions.

And when he had drawn her into his arms, those eyes had flashed until he was seared right through to his soul.

"Timothy, are you too busy to join us?"

He let his gaze be caught by those incredible eyes once more as he savored the sight of Serenity standing in the doorway. Her bright red spencer was buttoned to her chin beneath her sedate black cloak. Pale fur edged its hood, brushing her cheeks as he wished his fingers were.

"Us?" he asked.

"Theodora and I are going into the village to watch the mumming play that is to be held on the green this afternoon."

"Grandfather gave his permission?"

She laughed. "His blessing, to own the truth."

"Blessing?"

"He said it would be a blessed relief not to have Theodora teasing him about it endlessly." She smiled. "It seems that she has learned a lot already from other children about how to be a child and get her way."

"It seems that she has learned a lot about how to beguile a gentleman into giving her what she wants." Standing, he closed the book. "Your teaching, I assume?"

"Have you found a way to get your new factory back to the schedule you had planned?" she asked, noting the gold letters set into the leather binding: *Cheyney Enterprises*.

He shook his head and took her hand as he led her toward the door. "Not yet."

"If you must work—"

"I *must* escort you and Theodora to watch the mumming play, or I swear she will tease me until I do so. If she could change Grandfather's mind on this, I stand in awe of her powers of persuasion." As he closed the door behind them, he brought her to face him. "Although I suspect she had help from another whose powers of persuasion would be enough to turn any man's head, no matter his age."

"I am glad your grandfather heeded me."

"As I am."

When he kissed her lightly before taking her hand again as they walked along the hall, she smiled. She had no idea where this afternoon might lead, but she could not wait to find out.

Serenity took Theodora from her nurse. Nestling her in the blankets on the sleigh's seat, she drew another around her.

"Are you comfortable?" Serenity asked.

"Yes." Theodora beamed in anticipation.

"Are you warm?"

"Not as warm as Timothy, I collect."

Serenity glanced at Timothy, who was walking toward them, his heavy coat slapping his boots. When he chuckled, she knew he had heard Theodora's words.

"My heaviest coat," he said with a grin.

"I am glad to see you have decided to be sensible," Serenity replied, "rather than fashionable."

He plucked at the bulky wool. "I despise this coat. It weighs about as much as the curtain wall, and it smells from being in storage."

"You will appreciate it before the afternoon is over."

"I hope you are more sure of that than I am."

"I am," Serenity said. "That is why I asked Henry to have it ready for you."

Theodora giggled as Timothy handed Serenity in to sit on one side of her before walking around the sleigh and getting in on the other side. "Are we all set?" the little girl asked.

"As soon as you make a promise to me," he replied with a grin.

"What promise?"

"You must not tell the mummers if they do something wrong." He gave her a mock frown as he slapped the reins on the back of the horse.

Theodora laughed again when the sleigh slid with a soft whisper through the snow. "How will I know if they do something wrong? I have never seen them before."

"Ah, but I know you have convinced Serenity to find you that book with all the pictures showing mumming plays."

"I read it." She smiled up at Serenity. "Almost all by myself."

"*All* by yourself. If that one page had not been ripped and caught on the next page, you would not have needed me to help at all." Serenity stretched her hand along the back of the seat to put her fingers on Timothy's sleeve. "Your invention works perfectly."

"I should have thought about doing something like that a long time ago," he said.

"You should have," Theodora said in a tone that she had borrowed from her great-grandfather. "But Aunt Ilse said there is no inspiration that works better for a young man than having a beautiful woman by his side." She paused, then asked, "What was she talking about?"

"Aunt Ilse meant," Timothy said quietly, "that any man would do anything to win a smile from you or Serenity."

"Anything?"

He chuckled. "You minx. Almost anything, I should say, before you have me swimming the Channel to bring you something back from Paris."

"I do not want something from Paris. I want to see the mumming play."

Serenity smiled at the little girl's certainty, and she smiled even more broadly when they stood together on the green in the midst of the village. The simple houses edging the green were bright with candles that reflected on the strips of paper disguising the mummers. As the men acted out battles, with one falling and being brought back to life by a doctor character, Theodora cheered along with the other children. Even the speeches by the participants, each representing a different historical or legendary character, brought grins from the youngsters. The plays came to an end with a sword dance performed by six men.

Serenity watched, fascinated, as the men began in a circle. The swords were balanced on the men's shoulders, each man holding on to the sword of the man in front of him. As the patterns were created and then taken apart to make new ones, the men continuously held the swords in a steel cat's cradle. Dancing together and apart, they finished all linked together with the swords in a star pattern around the shoulders of one man in the middle. She cheered with the others and wondered how long she had held her breath, fearing that even a single gasp could destroy the perfection.

As they climbed back into the sleigh to return to Cheyney Park, Theodora prattled with excitement, reliving every moment of the play as if neither Timothy nor Serenity had been present. She giggled so hard that half of her words were incomprehensible.

"I think she enjoyed herself," Serenity said, chuckling as she sat beside Timothy, letting Theodora lean her good arm on the side of the sleigh.

"Proving that you are right once again." He grinned as he slipped one arm through hers and picked up the reins.

"I am glad I was."

"So am I."

She tipped her head to his shoulder as he steered the sleigh out of the village. While he teased Theodora, telling her that he was going to make her a hat covered with strips of paper like the ones the mummers had worn, she closed her eyes and let happiness envelop her. She could imagine few things more wonderful than spending an afternoon with him like this. Her lips tilted in a soft smile. The things she could imagine that would be even more spectacular should not be filling her head, but she could not halt the images of how his eyes closed in the moment before his lips found hers for an eager kiss.

"Look!" cried Theodora.

Serenity raised her head, wishing she could have had a few more moments amidst the pure happiness. "At what?"

"At the window where Aunt Ilse put the tree."

She could say only "Oh!" as she gazed up at the house on the top of the hill. At a trio of windows, she could see the lights of the candles that had been tied to the branches of the evergreen tree. Through the uneven glass, the light flowed out to mingle with the snow.

"It's beautiful," Timothy said. "Now I can understand why she was so excited about this."

"Can I see it up close when we get back?" Theodora asked.

"Of course." Serenity smiled. "After all, you helped make the fruit strands that—"

The horse shrieked as it rose to two feet. Beside her Timothy cursed, fighting to keep the horse from bolting. Metal screamed even more loudly than the horse. The sleigh shivered.

The horse whinnied again as leather snapped and flew about like a madman's whip. Serenity pulled Theodora closer to her as the sleigh bucked like the horse. She heard Timothy shout something. She did not have time to understand his words as the sleigh tipped wildly to the left. Wanting to grip the seat, she could not. She must not let go of Theodora.

The sleigh slid backward on the hill as the horse broke away. The runner struck a bush. As the sleigh tipped again, it bounced.

Serenity shrieked, but refused to release Theodora. She struck the snow and the rock-hard earth beneath it. In her arms, Theodora moaned, then began to cry. If the child had broken something . . .

"Theodora! Are you all right?"

The little girl brushed snow out of her eyes. "Is the horse hurt?"

Serenity sat up and lifted Theodora to sit. "The horse should be fine and halfway back to the stables by now. How are you?"

"I bumped my head."

"I see." She tipped back the child's hat to discover a ruddy spot the size of her thumb. "Anywhere else?"

"I lost my glove."

Serenity patted the snow to find the missing glove. Picking it up, she knocked snow from it and placed it back on Theodora's hand. "Sit right here. I want to see where Timothy is."

"No wolves will eat me, will they?"

"If I see any, I shall tell them that you taste horrible. All right?"

Theodora grinned. "All right."

Serenity's smile vanished as she pushed herself to her feet and stared at the upended sleigh farther down the hill. Where was Timothy? She had thought he would come running to make sure she and Theodora were not badly hurt.

Pressing her hand over her mouth to keep her gasp of horror from escaping, for it was sure to upset Theodora, she rushed down the hill to where a dark form was stretched out on the snow. Only half a form, she realized, because the rest of it was beneath the sleigh, which was tilted at a peculiar angle.

She dropped to her knees in the snow. Brushing Timothy's hair back from his eyes, she whispered his name. Theodora shouted to her from up the hill, but she did not answer as she stared at his face, which was smoothed out as if he were asleep. Sweet heavens, he was not dead, was he?

She slipped her fingers beneath his high collar to seek his pulse. With a yelp and an oath, he opened his eyes and pushed her hand away.

"I am just trying to see if you are alive," Serenity said.

"Try doing that without pushing snow down my collar next time, if you would." He grimaced. "Dash it! I cannot move my legs."

"You have a sleigh on top of them."

"The sleigh?" Timothy looked past Serenity's worried face to see the lurking bulk of the sleigh behind her. He tried to slip his legs from beneath it, but they were securely pinned.

"Do not move," she cautioned. "If you have had the misfortune to break a bone—"

"Which I have not. There's no pain."

"Sweet heavens! If you cannot feel anything—"

He caught her hands in his. "Serenity, I am fine. I am simply stuck."

"Stuck?" She gasped.

"It seems that way. The runner must have broken off and twisted around my legs. I can wiggle my toes, and I can feel the sleigh above my boots. I simply cannot extract my legs from beneath the sleigh." He grinned wryly. "It is a most ignoble sensation to be stuck like this."

"Mayhap I can help."

"Don't be want-witted. That sleigh is heavy, and the blades were sharpened before we left Cheyney Park. You could hurt yourself." He glanced around. "Where is Theodora?"

Serenity pointed up the hill. "She is there. We were thrown clear before the sleigh crashed and broke."

"For the second time, you have been thrown clear." He caught her hands again as her eyes dimmed. "Forgive me, Serenity, for reminding you of *that* accident when you must be so unsettled from this one."

"How could I not think of that one? But at least we are all alive and hurt no worse than a few bruises."

"And stuck."

Finally he was rewarded with a smile from her. Although his head ached as if both the sled and the horse had run over him, he slipped his arms around her and drew her down to meet his lips. Her hands clenched on his shoulders, and he tasted desperation on her lips. Not desperation, but fear. For him and for Theodora, he knew. As his gloved hands edged along her back, bringing her closer, he cared only for the caress of her slender body against him.

Pulling back, she whispered, "Timothy, we should not be doing this. Theodora is here."

"And she can see that there is nothing we can do save kiss when almost half of me is under this sleigh."

Her smile was clearly reluctant, but it rose to her eyes when he squeezed her hand before kissing it lightly. "I should get some help, Timothy," she whispered.

"Yes, you should." He chuckled. "It is getting as cold as the devil's heart lying here in the snow." He ran his fingertip along her cheek. "It could be warmer if you were lying here beside me."

"Where I would be as safe as a babe in its mother's arms."

He lowered his voice to a husky whisper, "Don't be so certain of that, sweetheart."

Color soared up her cheeks as her mouth grew round. Stumbling to her feet, she stuttered, "L-let me g-g-get Theodora." She took a deep breath, giving him a most intriguing view from the ground. "I shall send help as soon as I can get to Cheyney Park."

Timothy rested his chin on his folded arms and watched her skirts swaying as she hurried back to where Theodora was sitting. When she gathered the little girl up, he expected her to rush on. Instead, she turned and came back down the hill.

"Cheyney Park is at the top of the hill," he said, trying to sound cheerful. It was getting dashed cold beneath this sleigh. The wind was rising again, and he did not want to get out from under the sleigh just in time to discover his toes were frozen. He knew, as well, that if the sleigh shifted, it could fall down on him and shatter his legs. Even though he had been careful to say nothing of that to Serenity, he guessed she knew that, too.

"Theodora insists on staying here with you," Serenity replied.

He shook his head. "Theodora, it is too cold. Let Serenity take you home."

"No!" the little girl said with rare fervor. "Timothy, you sit with me when I cannot move. I want to sit with you when you cannot move."

Timothy looked from the child's determined scowl to Serenity's face, which softened from shock to gentle amazement. Like him, she must not have guessed that Theodora's heart was greater than her small body. He started to speak, but his voice cracked. He began again. "Theodora, it will not do you a bit of good to sit in the snow and get cold."

"I read a book where a man froze to death in the snow. He just got sleepy and never woke up." Her jaw jutted with a resolve that reminded him of his grandfather. "I will sit with you and talk to you so you will not go to sleep and freeze to death."

"I cannot talk her out of it," Serenity said softly. She set Theodora on top of him.

"What are you doing?" he asked. If this was her idea of a way to help him, he did not want to ask whom she would seek to come here to move this sleigh, for he feared she would bring the tiniest maid in the kitchen.

When she drew off her coat, he started to chide her; then he realized what she was planning. She set the coat on the snow and put Theodora on it. Pulling it up around the child, she buttoned the topmost button to hold it in place around her shoulders.

"Hurry!" Timothy urged, his concern now for Serenity, who was already shivering as the icy wind tugged at the fine material of her gown.

"I will." She turned, then smiled at them. "Don't go anywhere."

Theodora laughed, and Timothy put his chin back down on his arms. He let a grimace thread his forehead as Theodora watched Serenity run up the hill toward Cheyney Park, but had a smile in place as soon as the little girl looked back at him. He had not been completely honest with Serenity. There was a pain climbing his left leg that gave him sympathy for a beast caught in a trap.

"You are not sleepy, are you?" Theodora asked.

"No, just cold."

"Cold is good when you do not want to freeze to death."

He chuckled in spite of the thickening ache in his leg. "I suspect you are right."

"I am." Theodora raised her chin. "I read it in a book."

"And you like to read?"

"More than anything." She shook her head. "No, I like being with you and Serenity more."

"We like being with you."

Her eyes brightened. "I am not just a burden to you?"

"What gave you that idea?"

"I heard . . ."

Timothy started to frown, but halted when tears filled her eyes. Quietly he asked, "Theodora, who did you hear say something that would make you think that?"

"Uncle Felix and Uncle Arnold were talking, and I heard them say that Serenity is trying to prove that she is a saint by treating me as she does. That she is trying to impress Grandfather, and she is wasting her time because it shall not do her a bit of good."

"You heard all that and never mentioned it to anyone?"

She nodded.

Wondering what else the child had chanced to hear because the family had dismissed her to her lonely corner until Serenity brought out the sparkle in the little girl, Timothy said, "Your Uncle Felix and Uncle Arnold are wrong. Serenity likes to spend time with you because she likes you. I do, too."

"You do?"

"Yes." He clenched his teeth as another sliver of agony rose along his leg. "If Serenity has impressed Grandfather, it is because he sees that she cares for you."

"And for you."

"Yes," he said again, but more slowly. Not wanting to continue this conversation when he might let the pain betray him into saying something he should not, he added, "Tell me a story."

"What story?"

"How about one that you have read lately that you really enjoyed?"

"Telling stories is for bedtime, and you cannot go to sleep."

"Then tell me an exciting story that will keep me wide-awake."

Theodora nodded and launched into some tale that was so convoluted that Timothy lost track of it within seconds. He did not care. He simply listened to the rise and fall of her voice. The pain in his leg came in waves as well. When he heard a creak, he glanced up, but the wind was not strong enough to topple the sleigh to crush him.

Giving Theodora another smile so she would not be upset, he urged her to continue her story. He tried to ignore how her teeth chattered as she spoke. Glancing past her, he saw no one. As snow began to swirl around them on the rising wind, he hoped Serenity would be quick. He did not want to think of what would happen if she was delayed even a minute too long.

FIFTEEN

Serenity pulled the thick cloak more tightly around her as she ran along the road. How much farther could it be? She blinked as pellets of snow struck her, but she refused to bend her head. She did not want to miss her first sight of Timothy and Theodora.

She gasped with relief when she saw them huddled by the overturned sleigh. Rushing to it, she knelt by him as she had before. Cradling his head in her arms, she looked at Theodora and said, "They are coming."

"Who?"

"The men who will take you home where it is warm," she said, trying to keep her fear out of her voice. Why had not Timothy said anything to her? His skin was icy, and she did not want to think help was arriving too late.

Shouts raced down the hill before a crowd of men from Cheyney Park rushed up to the sleigh. Timothy groaned and opened his eyes as they peeked under the sleigh. She wanted to cheer that he was still conscious, but said nothing as the men peered all around the sleigh as they tried to figure out the best way to lift it away from him without doing further damage.

"Miss Adams," said the man she knew was the head groom, although she could not recall his name, "you and Miss Theodora must move away. We do not want to chance the sleigh falling onto you."

"All right." She scooped Theodora up into her arms. The little girl shivered and nestled against her. Drawing the cloak around her, she smiled her thanks when one of the lads tucked her coat up around Theodora.

"If you will go with Ned," said the head groom, pointing at the lad beside her, "he will see you back to the house while we get this off Lord Cheyney."

"I am not leaving. If—"

"Go!" ordered Timothy in a strained voice. "Theodora needs to get inside and out of the wind right away. We shall be right behind you."

Serenity wanted to argue, but saw by the tense expressions on the men's faces that she would be wasting her breath and the time they could be using to free Timothy. Nodding, she held Theodora close as she went back to the house with Ned. The lad put his hand at her back to guide her up the steep section.

The front door was thrown open as Serenity came up the steps. Branson held out his arms for Theodora as he asked about Timothy. She gave him some quick answers, but urged him not to delay. Theodora was too quiet as the butler rushed her up the stairs to her rooms, where Serenity had ordered a hot bath to be ready for her. Another should be waiting in Timothy's chambers.

She jumped aside as a maid hurried past her, carrying a steaming container. She had not ordered a bath for herself, but she would as soon as she knew Timothy and Theodora were warm. Following the maid up the stairs, she did not pause when Melanda called from near the banister rail. She had no time for a parade of silly questions. Once she was sure that Theodora was fine, she would come back and wait for Timothy to be brought back to the house.

Melanda frowned when Serenity did not answer her. She pushed away from the railing and hurried toward the room where she knew Felix would be at this hour. He always enjoyed some brandy before dinner, especially now that Theodora had joined them, upsetting the evening meal with her childish comments.

Throwing open the door to the cozy room where a fire flickered on the black marble hearth, she ran to where he was sitting in a leather chair, his feet propped up on a petit-point stool, a glass of brandy by his side. She guessed he had been here a while, because the bottle next to the glass was almost empty and his eyes were bright as he came to his feet. He was steady on them. That was no surprise. She had never seen Felix show any signs of being altogethery even when he had been drinking for hours.

"Melanda," he said with a smile, "you look distressed. Not at seeing me, I collect."

She gave him her most flirtatious smile, the one he always liked. Today was no exception, for he gathered her close. "You know I am always delighted to see you." Her smile vanished. "I just overheard Serenity in the foyer."

"Anything of interest, or was she just filled with bibble-babble as usual?"

"Something most interesting. She and that child were bumped around when the sleigh crashed on their way from seeing the mummeries in the village."

"And Timothy?" His arm drew back. "He went with them into the village."

She dropped to the chair and reached for his glass. Taking a deep drink, she whispered, "He may be hurt. Serenity is not sure. Apparently he was caught beneath the sleigh when one of the runners broke."

"Hurt?" He cursed and walked to the window where he could see anyone coming to the front door. "I have always thought my cousin was a lucky man, but now I am sure of it. If he could survive that sort of accident, he must be the luckiest man alive."

Melanda arched a brow. "I thought you deemed him fortunate for having Serenity here."

"Luck had nothing to do with that. If you will recall, the five hundred pounds and all was *my* idea."

"I do recall that." She frowned. "I am not sure it was the best idea you have ever had. These tales about Serenity being Timothy's betrothed may make everything much more complicated in the long run."

"I have some ideas about that, too. I will share them as soon as I finalize them."

She rose and put her hand on his shoulder. "You are always brimming with ideas, Felix."

Facing her, he pulled her into his arms. "Ideas that you like very much."

"Very much." She drew his mouth down to hers.

When Felix stepped away with only the briefest kiss, Melanda pouted. He blew her another kiss as he went out of the room. As he closed the door, he saw her drain the brandy from his glass and reach for the bottle to refill it. He wanted to tell her not to fret like this about Timothy and Serenity, but that would be a waste of breath.

He kept his steps to an easy stroll, so it appeared as if he had just chanced to pass by the foyer when the door opened and Timothy came in, followed by a footman. His cousin, he noted, was able to walk, although he limped a bit.

Coming down the stairs, Felix paused at the bottom. "What have you done to yourself *now*, Timothy?"

Timothy's attempt to smile probably looked more like a grimace. Not that he cared. All he wanted was to be sure Theodora and Serenity were warm, as he wished to be. "I tried to drive the sleigh over myself. Fortunately the runner broke before it could slice through me."

Felix waved aside the footman and ordered, "Alert Lord Cheyney's valet to have a hot bath ready for him."

"Miss Adams has already arranged for that," Branson said, coming forward. "You are looking better than I had hoped, my lord, after hearing of your misadventure."

"Better than I had hoped, I must own." Timothy straightened his ripped coat and smiled. "I can manage the stairs on my own, especially when I think of the steaming water awaiting me. Are Serenity and Theodora all right?"

Branson gave him a grin in return. "Miss Theodora is with her nurse and enjoying a warming bath. Miss Adams should, by now, be doing much the same."

"Good." He turned away before the butler or his cousin could see his reaction to the thought of Serenity naked and sleek in her bath. How much more quickly he would be warmed by going in to watch her bathe! No water, not even if it boiled, could heat him as swiftly as that single thought.

Although he wanted to race up the stairs and into Serenity's room to enjoy that sight, Timothy took the stairs slowly. The ache in his leg remained, and he understood why now that he had seen the long scratch where the sleigh's runner had collapsed on it. By the time he spoke with Serenity, he wanted to be walking as if nothing had ever been amiss.

"You are limping!" Not caring what anyone thought about her speaking to him when she was dressed in her gold wrapper with her hair pulled back by a single bow, Serenity ran into Timothy's sitting room.

Timothy smiled tightly as he looked past her. She glanced over her shoulder to see his valet by the door.

"Henry," Timothy said quietly, "I believe Miss Adams wishes to speak to me in private."

Henry nodded and closed the door to the hall. He bowed his head toward Serenity as he crossed the room and went through another door.

Her eyes widened when she realized that the second door led to a bedchamber. She had not guessed that Timothy's office was connected to his private rooms. Shaking her disquiet about her reputation from her head, she grasped Timothy's arm and steered him to a burgundy settee near the hearth.

"Sit," she ordered. "How badly are you hurt?"

He brought her to sit beside him. "It does not look as horrible as it feels. Just a very deep scratch and a bruise that would label me a hero if anyone were to see it." His smile disappeared as he added, "If you had not insisted I wear a heavy coat, I might have lost my leg."

"Oh, no!"

He drew her hands down from her mouth and folded them between his. "That did not happen, Serenity, thanks to you. I shall be walking around like a peg-leg pirate for the rest of the day and mayhap even tomorrow, but, by the time Grandfather's ball arrives day after tomorrow, I hope I shall be able to spin you about the room with no excuse for stepping on your feet, save for my own lack of grace."

She tried to smile, but it was impossible. Caressing his windscraped cheek, she whispered, "I would be glad to sit and watch the others, if that is what is necessary."

"Nonsense! How else can I see the envious expressions on the faces of all the other men if I do not twirl you about the room?" He smiled. "I am fine, sweetheart. Really, I am."

"I did not want to leave you lying there beneath the sleigh. I thought . . ." She buried her face against his chest, unable to speak the horrible words that revealed her deepest fears. To lose even a moment of the short time they had left together seemed the greatest tragedy she could imagine, even more catastrophic than losing her past.

His lips touched her hair before he whispered, "It is over. You and Theodora suffered no more than a few bumps and having your wits scared out of you. My injuries are not much more serious."

Looking up at him, she asked, "What happened? Why did the sleigh overturn?"

"It clearly had a weak spot. When the horse was frightened and bolted, one of the runners collapsed. Fortunately the road was bumpy, so you and Theodora were thrown out before you could be badly hurt."

"Frightened horse? What frightened the horse?"

"I did not see, but something must have, because it was doing fine until it let out that cry."

She rose and rubbed her hands together. They were so icy not even his touch could warm them. "I do not like this, Timothy."

"I should think not. It was a harrowing experience."

"No, that is not what I mean. I do not like the fact that I have been in two vehicles that were upset in such a short time."

"I should think not." He surged to his feet, then winced. Waving aside her gasp of dismay, he asked, "Are you suggesting that these two incidents might be related?"

Serenity hesitated, then shook her head. "That is silly, I know. I am unsettled from this, and I am not thinking clearly. The carriage accident was several weeks ago and miles from here."

"You are upset." He took her hands in his again. "Let us speak of something else."

"What would that be?" She smiled as his touch broke through the ice clamped around her heart, easing that cold more than her bath and thick wrapper had.

He pulled her up against him. "Of how each man in Cheyney Park shall wish he could be me when he watches me whirl you about in my arms." When he started to turn her about as if they were waltzing, he groaned.

"Sit," she urged, steering him back to the sofa. "You should be resting instead of trying to jest me out of my dismals."

"I had enough rest in the snow." Despite his words, he sat and let her lean him back against one arm. He was silent as she went to the bedroom door.

At her knock, Henry opened it. His eyes became round when she told him what she wanted, but he brought her several pillows from the bed. Thanking him, she closed the door before coming back to the settee. She put one pillow under Timothy's leg and reached to put the other behind his head.

Taking the pillow, he tossed it to the floor. She gasped when he caught her wrists and drew her down toward him. His fingers swept up her back to bring her mouth to his. The desire she had seen in his eyes when he was lying in the snow she now tasted in his kiss. When she leaned across him, his heart thudded beneath hers, the most delicious melody she had ever heard.

She laughed when he sprinkled kisses across her cheeks, but when he caught her face between his hands and tilted it so his gaze held hers, she saw an intensity she never had before in the depths of his eyes.

"What is it?" she whispered. She did not want to do anything to bring this moment to an end. Too many of their other kisses had been intruded upon or come to a swift end. She wanted this to continue until she wanted no more, which she guessed would be a time that would never come.

"Felix tells me I am a want-witted beef-head," he answered in a low voice.

"Does he?" She watched her finger trace his beguiling lips. "And why does he say that?"

"Because he thinks only a want-witted beef-head would resist sampling every pleasure a beautiful woman like you could offer him."

Her eyes wide, she drew back. He kept his arms around her, so she could not stand. Slowly he leaned her back over him again.

"He is right," he whispered. "I *am* a want-witted beef-head, because I do want you, Serenity."

"Timothy, you know this is just a game."

"Is it?" He gathered her close to him as he murmured against her hair, "Is it, sweetheart?"

"Yes." The word slipped past her lips in a breathless moan when his tongue teased her ear.

"Then it is a game where we both can be winners." His hands framed her face once more as he pressed her mouth to his.

A scream came from behind Serenity. Leaping to her feet, she stared at Mrs. Scott, who stood in the doorway. The housekeeper stormed into the room just as the other door opened, and Henry rushed out.

"My lord!" Mrs. Scott chided, wagging a finger at him as if he were a child. "I would think you cared more for Miss Adams than to treat her like this."

Timothy smiled as he pushed himself up to sit. It never had been proven that the housekeeper had a system of spies throughout the house, listening at keyholes, but he suspected that Grandfather was correct in surmising that she did. "Mrs. Scott, I am kissing Serenity because I *do* care for her."

"Don't try to trip me up with your wit, my lord. You know what I mean."

"Her reputation, do you mean?"

"Exactly." She crossed her arms in front of her, her foot tapping against the floor. She included an abashed Henry in her glower, but the valet wisely said nothing.

"I have to say I was not thinking of anything but her sweet lips at the moment, Mrs. Scott."

"I would say that is shameful, my lord."

"Would you deprive me of the very best medicine that is sure to get me back on my feet?"

The housekeeper looked down at him, her toe striking the floor even faster. "On your feet is not your goal, my lord, if I may say so."

"It seems you have." He laced Serenity's fingers through his and smiled up at her. When she smiled back, her eye closing in a lazy wink, he was startled. He had not guessed Serenity would find this so amusing. There was so little he knew about this fascinating woman—so little she knew about herself. He wished they had the time to discover it together.

Mrs. Scott frowned at both of them, but he saw the good humor in her eyes as she raised her hands in defeat. "What else can I say? It is not as if I have to force you to agree to do the right thing and marry her. You already have offered her marriage."

That was the wrong thing to say, he knew instantly, because Serenity stiffened beside him. When Mrs. Scott walked out, leaving the door open as far as it could go, he put his hand on Serenity's arm to keep her from leaving.

"Sweetheart—"

"Please do not call me that." She lifted his hand off her sleeve as she glanced at Henry.

"Henry," Timothy said, without pulling his gaze from Serenity's abruptly pale face, "you are excused."

"If you think that wise, my lord."

"I think it would be less wise for you to remain here just now."

"I understand." Henry's tone suggested exactly the opposite, but he hurried back into the bedchamber, closing the door in his wake.

Serenity flinched as the door shut. "I think I should go and check on Theodora."

"I will go with you.

"Timothy, I really want to be by myself. I am so confused."

Standing, he put his hands on her shoulders. All his amusement was gone. They had been interrupted too often. The house would grow only more crowded over the next two days as guests arrived for the birthday assembly and the New Year's celebrations. "I understand because I am confused as well. I know this betrothal is only . . ." He glanced toward the hall door.

Again her face grew pale. "Please let me go. Anything you or I might say now could be the careless word that ruins everything."

"Especially if we spoke of how wondrous you were in my arms."

"Timothy, this is senseless. All we will do is hurt each other more."

He knew she was right, but he also knew he could not let her walk away like this. Where had the line between charade and the truth gone? They were one and the same now, and he did not know what that was.

SIXTEEN

Serenity looked over her shoulder into the glass. The lacy train of her gown was matched by the white ruffles that edged the sheer fabric opening on the front of her gown to reveal the scarlet underdress. Silk flowers were woven through her hair and along the edges of her sleeves. At her throat, a necklace glittered with diamonds and rubies amid pearls.

"You look so lovely, Miss Adams." Nan rocked from one foot to the other, unable to hide her excitement.

"Thanks to your help." She touched her upswept hair. "You have a true gift for doing hair, Nan."

"I enjoy it." She giggled, sounding as young as Theodora. "I practice on the kitchen maids when Mrs. Gray is not watching."

"I shall keep your secret."

She dampened her lips and said, "I would like to continue being your abigail after you and Lord Cheyney are married." She gulped. "I hope I was not too presumptuous to ask like this."

"Not at all." Serenity rubbed her hands together, then took the fan her abigail held out to her. The web of half-truths seemed to be closing in around her more every day. "I will speak with Mrs. Scott about your desire to continue serving as an abigail."

There! That was the truth. Even if Nan could not continue to serve her, the young woman might be able to assist any guests who called at Cheyney Park until Theodora was old enough to put aside her nurse and need an abigail's attentions. It seemed wondrous to speak the truth.

Then why was she so reticent to tell Timothy what was in her heart?

Serenity hurried out of her rooms, hoping to avoid having to answer that question. As she came down the stairs to the floor where the ballroom doors had been swung wide open, Timothy stepped out of the shadows of the stairwell and held up his hand to her.

She stood, frozen on the stairs, as she admired the way the candlelight gleamed off his golden hair and emphasized the breadth of his shoulders in his coat that was the same scarlet as her underdress. Unblemished white breeches and a waistcoat with holly and ivy embroidered across its front were the perfect complement to his smile.

"How beautiful you look," he said, as she convinced her feet to carry her the rest of the way down the stairs.

If only she could persuade her tongue as easily not to want to speak of how she loved him. . . .

"You are in prime twig yourself, my lord."

He took her hand and raised it to his lips. Through her lacy gloves, the heat of his mouth warned her that the blaze of desire burned as hotly in his eyes. He curled her fingers over his as he murmured, "I considered wearing my work clothes, for no one shall take note of me once you enter the room."

"You are going to turn Serenity's head with such compliments," cooed Melanda from behind him.

Irritation flickered through Timothy's eyes, but it was gone as he turned to greet Melanda and Felix. They were, Serenity noted, wearing outfits that matched even more closely than hers and Timothy's, for the lace at Felix's cuffs was identical to what hung from Melanda's fan. As Melanda snapped it open and waved it in a motion that was sure to catch every eye, she smiled broadly.

"I fear," Timothy said, "that it shall take more than a few words to turn Serenity's head."

"And it seems you have found the very way."

"I have not seen much of you two for the past day," Timothy continued as if Melanda had not spoken. "When you did not join us for dinner last night, we were about to send out another search party for you. However, we decided panicking again would not be the wisest thing we could do."

Melanda scowled, then smiled as she slipped her arm through Felix's and leaned against his shoulder. "Felix and I had special plans yesterday."

"It is fortunate that those plans allowed you to return in time for Grandfather's party." Timothy grinned. "I think tonight's invitations are closer to a royal command than a request."

Felix said in a growl, "What else do you expect from Grandfather? He has no intentions of not having everything his way tonight."

"And why not?" asked Serenity. "He should have everything as he wishes for his seventieth birthday celebration. If I am fortunate to live that long, I intend to be just the same."

"Is that a warning, sweetheart?" Timothy laughed.

"Just a fact."

"One that I will keep in mind for the future."

Serenity's breath caught. A future? A future together for her and Timothy? Was that possible? She put both hands on his arm, wanting to believe this was real and not just one of the dreams that dared her to believe anything was possible when two hearts were brought together by love.

"First," Felix said in the same cantankerous voice, "we have to get through this night and all the congratulations and all the silly traditions of Cheyney Park."

Melanda's laugh contrasted with Felix's grim expression. Tapping him on the arm with her fan, she said, "Do not be in a pelter, Felix. Tonight is the culmination of all you and Timothy have planned. You should enjoy every moment of it."

"I should, shouldn't I?" Felix took her arm and steered her through the servants gathered at the top of the stairs, waiting for the guests to arrive.

Serenity frowned. "What is upsetting him?"

"Who knows?" Timothy shrugged.

"Do not let him ruin your evening."

"Felix's moods will not ruin my evening." He smiled more sincerely and offered his arm. "The guests will be coming down soon. Shall we take our places?"

Glad to do anything to escape her uneasy thoughts and even more elated to be by his side, she walked with him into the ballroom, which now was decorated with greenery. A huge log was set by the fire pit, ready for its lighting with the arrival of Christmas.

The earl walked into the ballroom, looking as fashionable as his grandsons, and grinning like Theodora, who was carried in by her nurse. Telling them that he would leave the greeting of the guests to Timothy and Serenity, he sat in a far corner of the ballroom with Theodora while the orchestra tuned their instruments and began to play.

As if it were a signal, the guests began to arrive just as the first song was finished. Many of them were already staying at Cheyney Park, but others had arrived during the day from nearby estates. Greeting each one by Timothy's side, Serenity wondered if she had ever been happier than she was on this Christmas Eve.

She tried to hide her smile as the guests glanced again and again, with dismay and curiosity, across the hall at the tree that was covered with candles and cookies and the long strands of dried fruit. She suspected each of them feared the tree would burst into flames at any moment. Only the children, who were drawn to it as if by magic, and Aunt Ilse seemed delighted with it. Aunt Ilse invited them to sit with her by the tree and sing some song that must be in German, because Serenity could not comprehend any of it. Mayhap it was the one Aunt Ilse had been singing when she and the household's children had decorated the tree. The children who had arrived in the past day had learned it quickly, with enough giggles to cause heads to turn as their elders made their way to the ballroom.

The peculiar tree was soon forgotten as the dancing began. Serenity smiled when Timothy told her, with a wry grin, that he had promised his aunt the first dance.

"Go ahead," she urged. "Enjoy it."

"But—"

"Don't worry," Lord Brookindale said as he came to stand beside Serenity. "I will keep watch so that no other young blade comes along and steals her from you upon the strains of the first waltz."

"I will hold you to that promise, Grandfather," Timothy said, chuckling. "I trust you will make sure no . . . shall we say mature blade does the same?"

"Go along with you." The earl laughed. "You have won Serenity's heart, and she seems not to be a woman given to *à suivie* flirtations, offering you her smiles one moment and me the next."

Serenity smiled. "You are quite mistaken, my lord. If I had chanced to meet you first—"

"Don't try to betwattle an old man." He wagged his finger at her. "Off with you, my boy. Your aunt is not a patient woman." As Timothy bowed and went to offer his arm to his aunt, Lord Brookindale shook his head. "You shall have to forgive the boy. Sometimes he acts as if he is stuck in his ways as an ancient donkey."

"He wishes to honor his aunt by partnering with her for the first dance."

"A noble gesture, but *I* would have tossed tradition aside and danced with the lady who makes my heart dance so fiercely that I cannot hide it from anyone."

Serenity fluttered her fan to ease the heat climbing her face. Not from embarrassment, but at the thought of Timothy's heart being filled with love for her as hers was for him. Could it be possible?

She could think of nothing else as she watched the dancers. One man did walk toward her, clearly intending to ask her to dance, but a frown from the earl sent him off in another direction. It was just as well. Serenity was content to sit and listen to Theodora prattle about the ladies' gowns and to watch Timothy move with the grace of a willow waltzing with a spring wind.

As soon as the dance was complete, Timothy walked over to the orchestra, said something to the conductor, then came to where they were sitting. "I am about to become the most fortunate man in all of England." He smiled as he picked up Theodora. Whispering in her ear, he laughed when she held her hand out to Serenity.

"And why are you about to become the most fortunate man in all of England?" Serenity asked.

"Because I am asking the two prettiest ladies in England to stand up with me for the next dance."

"Me, too?" Theodora dimpled.

"Of course." He lowered his voice to a conspiratorial whisper. "If you don't mind me dancing with Serenity, too."

The little girl giggled.

Serenity was not sure if her cheeks could hold her smile. As much as she wanted to be in Timothy's arms—and she could see from his expression that he wished the same—he was willing to share this evening's excitement with a little girl who had known so little excitement. She wanted to fling her arms around him and thank him for opening his heart to Theodora, who clearly adored him. Instead she took Theodora's hand and ignored the stares as she walked with Timothy out into the center of the floor.

The music for the country reel widened Serenity's smile even more. The simple steps were perfect for making Theodora feel a part of the pattern. As the other dancers lined up on either side of them, Serenity paid no mind to the whispers as she watched the joy gleam on Theodora's face as Timothy handed her to Serenity before he bowed to begin the first movement of the dance.

Then, taking Theodora in his arms, he crooked his elbow to Serenity to invite her to slip her hand through it. The effervescent melody swirled around them, but Theodora's exultant laugh was an even sweeter song.

In spite of Timothy's best efforts, he quickly missed one of the steps, unable to complete the pattern when he held Theodora. Serenity laughed and picked up the steps where she could. Soon they all were laughing, caring little about the pattern of the dance as they whirled about, to the little girl's delight.

Serenity clapped as the music ended. The rest of the dance pattern had disintegrated into infectious laughter.

Timothy bowed deeply to Serenity, then to the others, all the while balancing Theodora in his arms. "I am honored to have had this opportunity to have a chance to dance with the *two* prettiest ladies at Cheyney Park tonight."

"In all of England!" Theodora corrected with a touch of arrogance.

Serenity fought not to laugh, because the little girl was being serious. Holding out her hands, she took Theodora from Timothy and squeezed her. "Boasting is not a pretty trait, Theodora."

"It cannot be a boast when it is the truth," Timothy returned with a grin.

"You are spoiling her."

"And you, I hope." He put his arm around her waist as he walked with her back to where the earl was wiping a tear from the corner of his eye.

"Mistletoe!" cried Theodora suddenly, pointing toward the rafter over their heads. "You must be kissed, Timothy."

"And will you kiss me?"

She shook her head. "That is Serenity's job."

"Her *job*?" Timothy gave her a false fearsome frown and heard Serenity's sweet laugh. It sang through him like his favorite song. "Must you make the process sound so distasteful?"

"Kissing is kind of disgusting." Her nose wrinkled.

"You think so?" He took Theodora out of Serenity's arms and placed her on a nearby chair. Then he grasped Serenity's hand and twirled her up against him. "Does this look disgusting?"

As he bent to capture Serenity's mouth, he heard Theodora's giggle in the moment before his pulse thundered in his head. The need to taste more than Serenity's soft lips overmastered him as her fragrance washed over him. Not caring how many watched, he lured her tongue into a dance more intriguing than any they would share tonight. Her breath surged into his mouth as her fingers curled along his shoulders.

As he raised his head, he whispered, "The next waltz is for you and me alone, sweetheart."

She nodded, her eyes ablaze with the longing that haunted him during his restless nights when he could not sleep for wanting her in his arms.

Timothy quickly realized that even a waltz was not private enough for the moment he wanted to have with Serenity. He was aware of every eye turned in their direction and the heads bending as he passed by with Serenity in his arms. He did not need to hear the comments, because he had no interest in what his grandfather's guests were prattling about. He only wanted a moment alone with Serenity, a chance to ask her to reconsider and stay a while longer until they could sort out this jumble he had created out of the best of intentions.

As the dance ended and the orchestra began the music for a favorite north-country quadrille, he whirled her toward the door to the hall. Smiling, he said, "I am so glad you are here tonight, Serenity. I had not realized how desperately Cheyney Park needed a lovely hostess to bring such beauty and grace to an evening's gathering."

"Your aunt is here."

"Aunt Ilse left Cheyney Park because she wanted the quiet life of a German princess, which she found less constraining than her life as the daughter of an earl."

"Well, you have Melanda."

He gave an emoted groan as he drew her out of the ballroom and into the room where the tree glowed with the soft light of candles that had almost burned out. He closed the door behind them. Sitting her on the settee by the window, he filled two cups with the mulled cider sitting on the hearth. The luscious scents of spices and evergreen drifted through the room, flavoring each breath with Christmas.

Serenity took a sip of the cider as Timothy sat on the floor beside the settee, his elbow resting on the cushion beside her skirt. She pulled her gaze from his hungry one to admire how the candles reflected in the windows. "Now I understand why Aunt Ilse was so eager to have this Christmas tree. The candles look like a sky filled with stars, and the one on the very top is the Bethlehem star."

"You may be right." He grimaced. "However, I must own that I think it is bizarre to have a dead tree set by the windows in a parlor."

She slapped his shoulder lightly and laughed. "Mayhap your grandfather was not so wrong when he said you were getting as stuck in your ways as an old donkey."

"He said that, did he?" He plucked her cup from her fingers.

"What are you doing?"

"This." He hooked an arm around her waist and pulled her down to sit on his lap. Curling his fingers through her hair, he kissed her.

It was as if one of the candles had exploded within her, melting every bit of her resistance to him. She could not imagine anywhere else she would rather be than in his arms, his lips on hers.

Something clanged from somewhere beyond the walls.

"What is that?" She gasped, jumping up and looking around.

Timothy chuckled as he set himself on his feet. "The bell in the chapel. You will not notice it after the bell rings three or four hundred times."

"Three hundred times? The bell is going to ring three hundred times?"

"Actually it will ring eighteen hundred and eighteen times, one knell for each year since Christmas was first celebrated. It used to be done in Dewsbury, west of here, but when it was stopped, the tradition somehow came to Cheyney Park. There is talk of returning it to Dewsbury."

She put her hands over her ears as the clanging's resonance grew in volume until it seemed as if she stood within the bell tower near the back wall. "That poor lad shall be exhausted long before he reaches eighteen hundred and eighteen peals."

"All the young men in Cheyney Park take their turns. I used to look forward to doing it every year."

"I am surprised any of you can hear."

He drew her hands down and laced his fingers through them. "I can hear well enough to hear your heart speaking to mine, Serenity."

"I have tried to silence it."

"I am glad you have failed."

The door opened, and Aunt Ilse smiled. "Timothy, your grandfather wishes to speak with you right away."

"Certainly." He motioned toward the tree. "It truly is lovely, Aunt Ilse."

"I am glad you think so, too." She whirled away in a cloud of pink and white.

Timothy sighed. "I should go and see what Grandfather needs."

"I know."

His fingers swept across her cheek, then tipped her lips toward his mouth. His kiss was swift, but told her how he longed for so much more. When he released her, her knees wobbled, and she took a steadying step.

Her foot hit his cup, and the mulled cider pooled on the carpet. "Go ahead," she said with a grimace. "I will find someone to clean it up."

"I shall be waiting for you to dance as the bells end their tolling."

"Or before."

He nodded, kissed her again with luscious fire, and went out of the room.

Serenity followed, pausing in the hallway to signal to one of the maids. Telling the young woman what had happened, she grimaced again when she noticed the dampness in her left slipper. The cider must have seeped into it. She should change into other shoes.

She put her hand on the banister to rush up the stairs, not wanting to lose a minute of the evening's excitement. Her name was called.

Turning, she saw a footman. "Yes?" she asked.

"This arrived just now, Miss Adams. The messenger said it was for you, and that it should be delivered without delay."

"For me?" Her heart thudded with anticipation as she reached out to take the letter he held.

Could her sister and brother have found out where she was? She prayed they would never learn how she had begun to doubt their existence when Timothy's solicitor had visited school after school and found no sign of any children who had an older sister matching her description who might be in service in Yorkshire.

"Thank you," she managed to say as she went back to the room where the candles on Aunt Ilse's tree were guttering out even as the tolling of the bells became more enthusiastic.

Opening the letter, she realized before she had read more than a few sentences that this letter had not been meant for her, but instead for Timothy. She should find him and give it to him immediately. She knew that, but she could not pull her gaze from the words.

She sat on the settee as she read, *We have had no luck in finding the children you described, Lord Cheyney.* The words pierced right through to her heart. Mayhap Timothy's solicitor had not been able to find them because the children had been turned out already when the money she should have sent for their tuition failed to arrive. She did not want to believe that, but she was no longer certain of anything as she faced the past that she had put out of her mind when she was in Timothy's arms.

Serenity took a deep breath to steady her fingers. She should give this letter to Timothy, but her curiosity kept her reading. Suddenly she gasped and stared at words she could not have guessed would be in this missive.

After investigating the information you sent me, my lord, I must say that I firmly believe your Miss Adams to be, in truth, Miss Helen Loughlin. Miss Loughlin has recently been reported as missing along with two servants. Although they apparently vanished earlier this month, word of that has only recently come to my ears and the ears of her family, for they have been in Town. Only when she did not arrive last week as planned did they learn of her disappearance. Miss Loughlin and her servants were en route to a masquerade rout at Hess Court, not much more than a hard day's ride from Cheyney Park. At the time of her disappearance, it is believed that Miss Loughlin was dressed in the simple costume of an upper servant.

Serenity wanted to deny what she was reading, but as the letter went on to describe her in close detail, she knew it must be the truth.

Squeezing her eyes shut, she whispered, "Helen Loughlin? My name is Helen Loughlin. I am Hel—"

Hellie, come in! 'Tis time for your lessons, young lady. Your father will be angry if you do not finish your language studies before tea.

The voice rang through her head like the echo of the tolling bells. Mimi's voice. *Mimi!* Mimi had been first her governess, then her abigail. Mimi always fretted about the tiniest detail. That was why she had insisted that Miss Loughlin wear her costume on the way to the masquerade party, so she would not arrive late and be shamed not to be in costume.

Serenity pressed her hand to her heart, which seemed unable to beat. Mimi had been in the carriage with her. Mimi and Ralph, the footman who had had a *tendre* for Mimi for as long as Serenity could remember.

Tears burst from her eyes as a cascade of sobs surged into her throat. She dropped the letter to her lap as she wept. Mimi and Ralph were dead, dead and buried in graves with no names to mark them.

She gripped the edge of the cushions while memories trampled her, each one more determined than the last to remind her of the terror of the moment when the carriage had teetered at the edge of the road. The crack of the breaking wheel, the curses from Ralph, the scream of the horses.

Horses? There had been but one horse attached to the small carriage. If she had heard another, then there must have been another carriage or a rider on the road. Had her carriage swerved to miss it? She could not recall anything but that one moment they were laughing and talking, and the next was filled with horror and pain. After that, there was nothing but waking up in the inn.

And before the journey to the masquerade . . . No, the memories were still uncertain. Half-remembered snatches of conversation, odd fragments of faces and rooms which made no sense.

"Helen Loughlin," she whispered. The name, save for that one memory of Mimi's voice, was as unfamiliar as a stranger's. Would she ever remember what had been?

Mayhap something else in the letter would prompt another memory, the very memory that would tell her more about her life before the day the carriage accident had propelled her into this new life as Serenity Adams.

She quickly read the rest of the letter. The paper crinkled in her hands as she stared at the final sentence over the solicitor's signature. She wanted to believe she had misread it, but even after three readings, she could not mistake the words.

It was as you suspected from the onset, and I trust you will tell Miss Loughlin the whole truth if it becomes convenient for you to do so.

SEVENTEEN

The whole truth? If it becomes convenient?

Serenity did not want to believe what the words suggested. This was not the first letter Timothy had received from his solicitor on this subject, for he had mentioned at least one other. Only in retrospect did she wonder why she had not asked to see that letter to seek some clue that might bring back her memories. Had she been so caught up in falling in love that she had not wanted to know the truth? Had he been so caught up in falling in love that he had not told her the truth?

She lowered the letter to her lap and drew out a handkerchief to wipe her eyes. Knowing that the letter should have been delivered to Timothy instead of her changed nothing. The truth could not be hidden any longer. How long had he known—or suspected—that she was of the *ton*? Much longer than he had suggested during their conversation in the chapel earlier in the week. By the date at the top of the page, she knew this letter had been sent from London the day before that conversation.

"What is amiss, Serenity?"

At Lord Brookindale's voice, her head came up at the name that she should not answer to now. She was Helen. Helen Loughlin. How many times must she repeat that to herself before she became comfortable with the name that must have been hers all her life, save for the past few weeks? Odd that she had found it easier to accustom herself to being called Serenity than this name she had possessed all her life.

"I wanted some time by myself," she said. That was not a lie.

"By yourself? When you should be in the ballroom celebrating my birthday?" He lowered himself into a chair and snatched the letter from her lap.

"That is mine, my lord!"

"My lord?" His brows lowered. Holding up his hand, he ordered, "Do not lather me with any out-and-outers when I suspect this letter will confirm what I have guessed all along."

"You guessed—" She closed her mouth before she could betray Timothy further.

Wanting to come to her feet, Serenity twisted her handkerchief. *Serenity!* She could not rid herself of this name that did not belong to her.

The earl read the letter once, then a second time. He handed the letter back to her with a sigh. "You should have come to me with the truth right from the beginning, Ser—Miss Loughlin."

"But I did not know the truth, my lord."

As she addressed him formally again, he scowled, his bushy brows jutting toward her as fiercely as his chin. "But you knew that the boys were spinning a web of lies in hopes of trapping me in it."

"Timothy wanted only to avoid disappointing you." She stood. "He lost himself so much in his factory-building project that he gave no thoughts to his obligations to marry and obtain an heir. I assure you that his thoughts were all for doing nothing to ruin this birthday celebration."

"You need not defend him to me. I can see the truth quite clearly. My legs may have slowed down with time, but not my wits."

"I did not mean to suggest that."

He patted her hand. "I realize that." His thick brows suddenly rose. "Loughlin, did you say?"

"Yes, my lord."

"I would like to believe that the fact that your name is Loughlin is only a coincidence, but this is too much of a jumble for me to believe that." He pointed to the settee where she had been perched. "You should sit, Miss Loughlin."

She nodded, wondering again why it was taking her longer to become accustomed to her true name than it had to her false one. Although she knew she truly was Helen Loughlin, every fiber told her that her name was Serenity Adams. Lowering herself to the chair, she blinked back the tears that swarmed into her eyes.

"I assume," the earl said, "that this loss of memory you have suffered is the one facet of truth through the whole of this."

"Yes, my lord."

He scowled more fiercely at her formal address, but asked, "Do you recall anything of your family, Miss Loughlin?"

"I recall that my mother died when I was not very old. My brother and sister—"

"You are an only child, my dear." He took a deep breath and released it through his clenched teeth. "This tale of a brother and a sister that permeates this letter from our solicitors, I own that I do not understand it."

"There was a letter in my apron when I was rescued from the carriage accident. Felix gave it to me. He said . . ."

The earl nodded slowly as she gasped in disbelief and dismay. "No, do not lower your eyes. You do not need to hide the truth from me. I believe you were purposely misled, Miss Loughlin. Do you recall anything of your father?"

"Only certain things that he spoke to me about. I cannot recall his face. Is he alive?"

"Yes, he is alive and, last I heard, quite well. Your father is Sir Philip Loughlin."

"Sir Philip?" The name reverberated through her head. "Is he the Sir Philip who was your son's friend?"

"How do you know that?"

"Timothy told me how a man he called Sir Philip was his father's friend and helped him design the Chinese folly in the water garden."

Again the earl nodded. "We are speaking of the same man. His estate borders Robin Hood's Bay to the east of here. Although he seldom leaves his estate to go farther than Town now, which explains why you and Timothy never met as children, before he wed your mother, who was the younger daughter of a baron, he traveled often in the East. His knowledge of Eastern art and culture is unparalleled in England."

"That explains how I knew what I knew of the temple lions and chopsticks." Her eyes widened. "Did you suspect the truth when I knew about the temple lions?"

"It did plant a seed of suspicion in my brain." Again he sighed. "I sent a message to your father to ask him obliquely if his daughter might be missing. When I got no response from him, I decided my suspicions were wrong. Now I understand why I got no reply. The letter probably remains at his house, because there was no urgent request to forward it to Sir Philip wherever he might be." He looked back at the page she held. "The poor man must be beside himself with fear for you."

The letter crinkled again as she clasped her hands. "Can I send him a note right away?"

"Of course. As soon as it is written, I shall have it sent to him." A hint of a smile returned to his taut lips. "What better gift could he receive in this Christmastide than the return of his daughter?"

"Thank you," she whispered.

"One thing I still do not understand. Although Timothy may not have recognized you, for as I said I doubt if you ever met, because of your father's focus on his studies, Felix must have spoken to you during the calls his father made upon your father." Again he smiled. "Not that I am excusing Timothy from any of this, but I am baffled about why Felix did not identify you from the onset."

Serenity recalled how she had suffered that strange sense of having met both Felix and his father previously. Had their odd expressions when she was introduced to them as if for the first time been because they knew she might recall their earlier meetings?

"I don't know," she replied.

"I don't expect *you* to know, my dear, but I expect both Arnold and Felix to have a much better answer for me than that." He pushed himself to his feet. "They do not have a bumped head as an excuse for forgetting what I doubt Arnold shall ever forget."

"What is that?"

The earl refilled her cup with mulled cider, then took one for himself. "Your father, my dear, was foolish enough to let Arnold sit down at the card table with him. Your father graciously agreed to accept Arnold's chit for his losses. They were massive losses. Apparently one of the things your father learned during his travels was to judge those around him with ease while hiding his own thoughts. That is an inestimable skill while playing cards."

"And he still owes my father this money?"

He nodded.

"And if Timothy had seduced me as Felix urged him to—"

Lord Brookindale's oath silenced her. "I shall disown that boy completely. No debt between gentlemen should include a lady's honor."

She pressed her hand to her bodice. She recalled Felix's triumphant grin as he had entered the ballroom with Melanda this evening. Had he been so sure then of getting his vengeance that he was enjoying his victory even before it happened? She did not want to believe that Timothy would be a part of such a thing, but he had lied to his grandfather to serve his own needs.

"Do you mean that Felix wished to have me ruined to repay my father for besting his father at a game of cards?" she whispered.

"It looks that way, doesn't it?"

"To own the truth, I no longer know what to think about anything, my lord."

Sorrow filled his eyes. "My child, I hope you will come to call me Grandfather, as you once did."

"But—"

"'Tis no different than it was before, for you never had any intentions of marrying my grandson, did you?"

"No." She dampened her abruptly arid lips. When had she taken on Timothy's horrible habit of lying in an attempt to protect this dear man from the truth? If she told him how she had hoped Timothy would speak of the dream in her heart and ask her to become his wife on Twelfth Night, the earl would denounce her as an air-dreamer. Mayhap she was, for she had dared to believe that Timothy might truly love her, too.

Why had she convinced herself of that when everything around her had been woven of a tapestry of lies?

"If you wish to retire," the earl said, setting his cup on a table as a knock came at the door, "I will make your excuses to the guests."

"Thank you." She added nothing else as a maid hurried in to clean up the spilled cider, which Serenity had forgotten in the morass of discovering a truth she never had expected existed.

Serenity raced up the stairs to her room. Closing the door, she was glad to see Nan was nowhere about. Her abigail would not have guessed she would return so early from the evening's entertainments.

With a sob, she pulled the flowers from her hair. She opened the closet and grasped her cloak. Throwing it over her gown, she tied it at her throat. She kicked off her slippers and drew on her high-lows.

She rushed back out into the hallway. No servants were in sight, so she paused by Timothy's door and went in to place the letter on his desk. It should have come to him. Once he read it, there would be no need for her to leave him a note to tell him good-bye.

A sob burst like a wretched bubble from her lips. She did not want to leave him—and her heart—but she could not stay. If she discovered he had known more than he had told her about her past, she would be shattered beyond repair.

It was easier than Serenity had guessed to slip down the stairs without being seen. When she reached the foyer, she bit back an oath. She had not guessed that Branson would not be at his regular post. She should have realized he would be busy with a multitude of tasks for the ball.

She motioned to a footman, who was rushing across the foyer. He paused and asked, "Miss Adams, is something amiss?"

She wanted to bite her tongue as she prepared another half-truth, but she had no choice. "Is Branson nearby?"

"Yes, miss. One moment please."

Although she wanted to rush out the door and put all of this behind her, she waited in the foyer. She stayed in the shadows, not wanting to chance being seen by Timothy or someone else in his family. She had no idea what she would say to any of them.

Branson smiled as he came into the foyer. That smile faltered when his gaze alighted on her cloak. "The night is very chill, Miss Adams."

"I know." She did not add how much colder she found the lies that had enmeshed her. "Do you know a Sir Philip Loughlin who lives near Robin Hood's Bay?"

"Loughlin?" He nodded. "Yes, I know the name, Miss Adams. Do you wish to have a message taken there?"

"Is the house far?"

He shook his head. "Not far, miss. If you were to start at dawn, you would be there before sunset."

"Will you have a carriage brought around?"

"Now?"

"Yes, please."

"Miss Adams, if you plan to drive all the way to Robin Hood's Bay, you would be wise to wait until the morrow to begin."

She smiled tautly. "I cannot. Branson, will you please have a carriage brought?"

For a long moment she thought he would refuse, but then he nodded. "At least allow me to take a message to my lord for you."

"I have informed the earl of my plans."

Branson lost his usual smile as his face dropped into a frown. He must believe that she had misunderstood him, and mayhap that was all to the good. If the butler thought that she and Timothy had had a falling-out, Branson would not rush to Timothy with the tidings of her leaving. He would leave that horrible task to the earl.

The cold wind swirled into the foyer, bringing sharp flakes of snow with it as Branson sent a footman to have a carriage brought. The snow must be blowing up from the ground, because the stars pierced the sky with the intensity that they reserved for freezing winter nights.

More quickly than she had expected, but much more slowly than she wanted, a closed carriage was driven under the porte cochere. Bidding Branson farewell, she hurried down the steps and let the footman hand her into the carriage.

She pulled the cloak more tightly around her shoulders as she settled herself on the carriage's cold seat. She knew Branson's counsel had been wise. She *should* wait until dawn to travel, but she could not remain a moment more in that house amid the lies and counterlies.

Raising her hand to slap it against the side of the carriage, she took a steadying breath. She did not want to leave. She could not stay.

Her breath burst from her in a scream as her wrist was seized. She whirled on the seat to stare through the window. "Timothy!" she gasped.

"Where do you think you are going?" he demanded.

Serenity slowly lowered her hand. She said nothing as Timothy threw open the door so hard that it crashed against the side, and climbed into the carriage. He sat on the seat facing her.

"I was sure Mrs. Scott was mistaken when she told me that she had seen you stepping into a carriage in front of the house," he said, each word as icy as the night wind.

Mrs. Scott! She should have spoken to the housekeeper before she had taken her leave to allay Mrs. Scott's mind as she had Branson's.

"She was correct." She could keep her voice as emotionless as his, but she had to clench her hands in her lap to do so. Her fingers wanted to course along his strong face and slip up through the gold richness of his hair . . . just once more, while she believed that love was possible.

Love? Her heart was witless. This had been just a masquerade, with the greatest hoax being played upon her. She had believed she was doing something kind to help Timothy, but that kindness could have destroyed her father.

Her hands clenched in her lap. Why couldn't she see her father's face? Hints of his voice played through her head, but the words were ones an adult would speak to a child. No memories emerged from any time more recent than when she had been barely old enough to have a tutor.

"You did not answer me," Timothy said, his voice still harsh with barely repressed anger. "Where are you going at this hour?"

"I am going home."

"Home?" He stared at her as he whispered, "You have remembered who you are?"

"Not completely." Closing her eyes, so she was not tempted to soothe the emotions in his, she whispered, "All the answers you need are in a letter I left on your desk."

"You wrote me a letter and—"

"The letter is from your solicitor." She took a deep breath, then opened her eyes. She could not hide from the truth. "It was misdelivered to me, but it told me that I am, in truth, Helen Loughlin."

"Loughlin?" he choked, and she knew he had made the connection as swiftly as his grandfather had.

"It seems that your finding me was a most happy happenstance for your cousin, who may not have been as puzzled by the truth as I was."

Timothy cursed with rare fervor. "Of course he knew who you were. He and Uncle Arnold have called several times on Sir Philip in recent years."

"Enough so that your uncle owes my father a heavy debt." She looked down at her clasped hands. "But that is not important. What is important is that my father must be frantic with worry that his daughter is dead. I must not delay a moment longer going home to reassure him of the truth."

"Let me send a rider. The message will reach your father far more quickly than a carriage."

"Thank you, but no."

"You can leave on the morrow." He reached for her hands. "If—" He cursed again when she drew her hands away.

"I must leave now."

"At the very least, allow me to escort you home. You should not be traveling alone all night."

"Yes, you may escort me home." She held up her hand to halt him from replying before she had said all she must. "But only because I want you to assure my father that nothing untoward happened between us, in spite of your cousin's determination to see you enjoy the rights of the lord of the manor with me."

He slapped the side of the carriage to give the command to leave. The sound of the endless ringing of the bells grew fainter as he said, "I would never have done something to dishonor you, Serenity. I mean, Helen."

She looked down at her gloved hands again. "Mayhap it would be better if you addressed me as Miss Loughlin, my lord."

He grasped her hands. "Sweetheart, do not toss what we share aside as if it had no value."

"What value can lies have? They have no more substance than the colors of a rainbow, even though they are just as beguiling and seductive to the want-witted."

"'Tis no lie that when I hold you in my arms, I am certain that nothing in the world can be as wondrous. Then I kiss you and—"

"Timothy! No more!" She pulled away, edging to the far side of her seat. "I have been mired too long in lies, and I do not trust myself to know what is the truth any longer."

"I know what I did was wrong. Even doing what I did for a good reason was wrong."

She nodded. "Yes, it was."

"You will allow me no latitude on this, will you?"

"If I do," she whispered, leaning forward to cup his face in her hand, but pulling her fingers back before they could touch his rough skin, "my heart will demand the same latitude."

"Your heart?"

She did not dare to close her eyes, although she wanted to shut out the hope blossoming in his. If she shut her eyes, she doubted if she could keep the tears from slipping past her lashes. "Even though I knew it was ludicrous, I could not keep from falling in love with the man who cared so deeply for his grandfather that he would go against his principles and devise this story to make him happy."

"I have succeeded only in making everyone miserable, including you."

"You have given Melanda a great deal to crow about. She will deem this a first-rate theatrical put on solely for her enjoyment."

He rose enough to switch seats so he sat beside her. Putting his arm along the back of the seat, he whispered, "I care nothing about Melanda and how she rates the world about her, because she dares not allow anyone too near unless that one can advance her in some way."

"She seems to think that Felix is that one."

"She may change her mind when she learns of his scheme to ruin you and your father to get his vengeance." He tried to smile, but failed. "Or mayhap not. They are, as you have mentioned more than once, two of a kind." His voice grew somber. "We are speaking of Melanda and Felix when I wish to be speaking of us. Let them worry about their own future together. What of ours?"

She looked at him and whispered, "I don't know."

EIGHTEEN

$\mathcal{F}$elix reached for a glass of brandy. He needed something to ease the ache in his skull. Those blasted bellringers! That tradition would come to an immediate end on the day he became earl. A man should not face Christmas morn with the echo of endless ringing banging through his head.

"You look distressed, my love," Melanda cooed as she leaned over the back of his chair. Dipping her finger in his glass, she rubbed the brandy against his forehead. "Another headache?"

"Yes."

"You should not be suffering from a headache." She bent and kissed his cheek. "Not tonight."

He tipped the glass back and drained it. "If those accursed bells would just stop."

"You should be used to them by now." She laughed as she filled his glass again and came around from behind the chair to sit on its arm. Taking a glass, she poured some for herself. "A toast, Felix?"

"To what?"

She laughed at his grumble. "To us would be a good start."

"Start? Everything has come to an end. Nothing has gone as I planned." He took her hand and gave her a weak smile. "Almost nothing."

"You are too glum when you should be happy." She rested her cheek against his. "Your grandfather's guests are enjoying themselves, and I saw your father leaving the ballroom with Mr. Younger and Lord Edsley."

He groaned. "Dash him! Edsley has a certain skill with the devil's books that might cost my father dear."

"Edsley was well into his third bottle of wine." She gave him a sly grin. "I made certain that he had his choice of several more in the room where they had retired to play cards."

"What did I do to deserve you?" He chuckled.

"You shall be asking yourself that again when I tell you what I came in here to tell you."

He sat straighter. "Something more?"

"The very best of tidings. *She* is gone."

"She?" He scowled. Only two people created this abhorrence in Melanda's voice. "Theodora?"

"That beastly child?" Her nose wrinkled. "No, not her. *She* is gone."

"Serenity?"

She laughed and nodded.

"She is gone?"

Melanda rose and reached for another chocolate from the box set on the table by the window. "I just heard that Serenity skulked out of Cheyney Park like a thief not an hour ago."

"And Timothy?"

She raised hooded eyes toward him and smiled. "I let your grandfather's heir know that his erstwhile betrothed was on her way home."

"Home?"

"To Sir Philip Loughlin's country estate near Robin Hood's Bay."

Felix stood, swaying. He waved aside her hand. "She knows the truth?" He rubbed his eyes. "By all that is blue, how did that happen?"

Sitting in his chair, Melanda reached into her bodice and drew out a crumpled page. "Poor, dear Miss Loughlin. This letter was delivered to her in error. It seems your cousin has developed such a *tendre* for Serenity that he was determined to find out the truth about her past so he could put her mind at ease about who she was before you persuaded her that five hundred pounds was the proper price for her to play Timothy's supposed betrothed."

Snatching the letter, Felix scanned it. Melanda was wrong. This letter made it clear that Timothy had set the solicitors on a search for those blasted children within days of the carriage accident. When writing that letter that he had pretended to take out of the apron's pocket, Felix had been certain that Helen Loughlin would do as he suggested and take on the role of Serenity Adams if she thought some children were dependent upon her for their survival. Everything he had heard had convinced him that Helen Loughlin was as loyal and honest as her accursed father, so he had been sure she would take this bait.

She had, and so had Timothy. In his determination to repay "Miss Adams" for helping him, Timothy must have started this search for her nonexistent siblings. That search had led to the truth. *Too soon! Too blasted soon!* If the letter had arrived even a day or two from now, his revenge might have been assured. Now . . .

With a curse, he threw the letter onto the hearth. He did not wait to see it turn brown and catch fire. Why had not he invented some other tale that would have compelled her to help Timothy, yet would not have created this longing to find her fictitious brother and sister?

"She is gone, Felix," Melanda murmured, coming to her feet and draping her arms around his neck. "And so is Timothy."

"They will not get far. It was beginning to snow when I came in here." He scowled at her. "Why did you tell Timothy that she had left?"

"Did you want to see his face yourself?" She walked her fingers up his arm. When he shoved her hand away, she pouted and said, "To own the truth, I did not tell him. I overheard him talking to Mrs. Scott." She sniffed. "'Tis about time someone eavesdropped on *her*."

"Why did not you come to tell me right away?"

"I have." She ran her hand along his arm again. "Don't fret, my love. Everything has worked out just as you had hoped."

"Nothing has worked out as I hoped!" He peeled her arms off him and shoved them away.

"It must have in one way. Your grandfather is certain to be furious at Timothy for being a part of this scheme." Her nose wrinkled as she reached for another chocolate. "You know how the earl says he expects more from his heir."

"Yes, his beloved heir who must do no wrong, and his other grandson who can do no right."

"Oh, Felix, don't be petulant. What do you care?"

He stared at her as if he had never seen her before. "How can you ask that? After all I have done?"

"It has obviously failed. Timothy is sure to bring her back here, and then, being the honest trout that he is, he will go to your grandfather and confess the whole."

"Be quiet," he muttered, rubbing his aching forehead. He did not need Melanda's vexing comments now. He had to think—and think fast. Father would be outraged when he heard of the chain of errors that had unraveled the carefully arranged pattern of lies.

Grandfather . . . He gulped. Grandfather would disown both him and Father, because the old man had become as fond of the woman he knew as Serenity Adams as if she were his own grandchild.

He knew what he must do. He must not delay.

Snow pelted the road, and wind blew against the lowered curtains on the windows. When the carriage slid as the road grew steep, Serenity gripped Timothy's arm.

"We must turn around," he said quietly.

"Yes." She shivered with more than the cold. "Take me back to Cheyney Park."

Opening the door in the top of the carriage, he shouted an order to the coachee. "Stay calm," he added as he drew her into the curve of his arm while the carriage rolled to a stop, then began the slow back-and-forth to turn it on the narrow road.

"We are not far from where the other carriage fell from the road."

"I know." He tipped her chin toward him, although she could not see his face in the shadows. "Make me a promise."

"If I can."

"Promise me that you will not flee again. Promise me that you will let me take you home to your father."

She whispered, "Yes, but I already agreed to that. Why are you asking me to promise again?"

"There may be much more to this than I had first thought."

"What do you mean?"

"I mean that—" His voice became a roar as the carriage slid along the road like the sleigh when the horse had bolted.

This horse screamed in horror when the carriage continued to careen out of control down the road. She heard branches strike the side. No, not just branches, but another vehicle. What was happening? Had another carriage lost control on the icy road?

She buried her face against his chest, not wanting to think that she had destroyed her best chance at her future in this attempt to rediscover her past. Any answer was lost when she was thrown against the carriage wall. Pain seared her head; then there was nothing but the echoes of crashing.

Felix leaped down from the box. Yes, this was the spot. It had taken longer than he had expected to turn his carriage and hurry back here. The roads were even more slippery than he had guessed. If he had not taken care, he would have been the one with an out-of-control carriage.

Water splashed onto his best breeches, but he did not care. *Excellent!* This time there would be no mistakes, because he had done the deed himself. He should have learned from his father by now that depending on others led to slipshod results. A job that needed to be done should be done by oneself.

Yet that had not been possible before. It would not have been easy to concoct an excuse to leave London before Timothy on the way to Cheyney Park, but he should have found a way instead of letting others make a jumble of all this. When his father had learned that Miss Loughlin would be at the masquerade at Hess Court, Felix had known his chance had arrived.

That had been bungled, but not today.

He walked to the edge of the road. Trees were broken where the carriage must have crashed through. He did not have much time. Someone might see the beast and then come to investigate. But he would not leave this time without making sure the deed was done—and done completely.

Grimacing as his boots sank more deeply into the mud, he picked his way down the hill. He cursed when his feet slid out from beneath him, and he dropped to sit in the mud.

As he pushed himself to his feet, he heard behind him, "You will find nothing down there, Felix."

Serenity held her breath as Felix slowly faced Timothy. She did not share Timothy's certainty that his cousin would not have a weapon. Already Felix had shown that he would resort even to murder to achieve his aims. She did not want to believe that, as she knew Timothy did not, but unlike her, Timothy had not been knocked senseless in the carriage. He had recognized the driver of the other carriage, which had tried to push theirs off the road.

Felix grew pale, then said, "I had no idea you were out on this stormy night, cousin. I thought you would be busy with Grandfather trying to think up the toasts for everyone's enjoyment."

"You did not think I would be with Serenity?"

"I had heard—that is, Melanda told me that . . ." His face became ghostly as Serenity stepped out of the carriage to stand beside Timothy. Glancing at the wreckage at the base of the hill, he gulped so loudly it sounded like a gunshot in the silent woods.

"She told you that I left to seek my father," Serenity said, "to reassure him that I was alive and well, although I could not remember much about him." She glanced at Timothy, whose face in the light of the lantern held up by his coachee, Jenkins, was as tautly sculptured as the rocks in the low wall. "And she told you that Timothy offered to escort me home."

"You don't know what you are talking about!"

"But Ned does." Timothy motioned to the lad from the stables as Ned stepped into the small circle of light, his clothes frozen to him. He had been calming the horses. "Mrs. Scott overheard your conversation with Melanda and asked Branson to send Ned to warn us."

Felix's curse warned Serenity how deeply he despised his grandfather and his household.

"Ned's warning came nearly too late," Timothy continued. "If Jenkins did not have such skill in the box, you might have succeeded in killing us instead of simply hurting Serenity's head again."

"And knocked her memories back into her head?" he sneered. "Or has the whole of this been a way for the two of you to carry on your affair right under Grandfather's nose? He will not appreciate being made a dupe by your scheme."

"The scheme, as you should recall, was your invention." Timothy drew Serenity closer and pulled his thick cloak over her as the wind howled along the road. "Serenity recalls no more than she did an hour ago, save that you just tried to kill us."

"An accident!"

"Was it? Like the sleigh that you took with you when you supposedly went to retrieve your father's cravat? Or did you, instead, have the harness fixed so that it would panic the horse to the point that it would bolt, sending the sleigh out of control?"

Serenity stared at Timothy in disbelief. She had not guessed that he had such suspicions.

Timothy gave his cousin no time to retort. "I grew uneasy when Serenity seemed to recall too many things when her memory was loosened by your comments. It appeared the two of you had more in common than you, Felix, wished me to guess."

"You cannot prove that I did anything wrong!" he cried.

"No, I cannot, although a true gentleman would take responsibility for his mistakes." He folded his arms in front of him, looking like his grandfather when the earl refused to be countermanded. "It is no mistake to tell you that you would show a decided want of sense to return to Cheyney Park in the wake of this. Grandfather may not be as forgiving as I that you tried to murder me here." Looking at Serenity, he said, "And attempted twice along this road to slay Miss Loughlin. Men have hanged for less."

Felix's face became gray. "You would not send me to hang, would you?"

"I would not, but I cannot speak for our grandfather or Miss Loughlin's father." He pointed to the horse that Ned had ridden to warn them. "I suggest you take yourself posthaste to somewhere where Grandfather cannot find you."

"Where?"

"I understand that Colonel Coleman's regiment is being sent to India."

Felix mouthed the word *India*.

"That you are half a world away should be enough to persuade Grandfather not to follow you. I suspect Melanda will not be thrilled with such a posting, but she should have thought of that before marrying you last night."

Serenity turned to look at Timothy. Was he jesting? No, his face was without a hint of humor. She had not guessed that Felix and Melanda were being wed when they had not appeared for dinner last evening.

"I have no funds of my own to buy a commission," Felix mumbled.

"I suspected that." Timothy reached under his coat and drew out a piece of folded oilcloth. "I had intended to speak to you of this under more congenial circumstances, for I saw it as an opportunity for you to obtain the prestige you have never hidden that you wish could be yours. Inside this, you will find what you must do to get your commission in London, Felix. I have arranged for the funds to be transferred to the lieutenant who was selling his commission."

"Lieutenant?" He gasped. "You bought me a mere lieutenancy?"

Serenity bit her lip to keep from saying that it was more than he deserved after trying to kill his cousin so his father might inherit the title and Felix after him. Only because Timothy knew how this would hurt his grandfather was he trying to settle the whole of this with little fuss.

When Timothy said nothing, Felix slowly took the packet. He walked to the horse and mounted. No one spoke as he vanished into the storm.

"But, my lord," Jenkins said, "London is in the other direction."

"My uncle's house will be his first stop." Timothy shook his head. "I shall have Melanda meet him there so they can travel to Town together." Putting his arm around Serenity, he said, "Now we can continue—"

A horse burst out of the darkness, racing straight toward them. Serenity screamed as Timothy shoved her up against the carriage, protecting her with his body. Who else wanted to see them dead?

"Lord Cheyney!"

At the shout, Serenity looked past him to see the rider reining in. It was not Felix, intent on another plot to kill them, but another of the lads from the stable.

"What is it, Louis?" Timothy asked.

"Lord Brookindale sent me to find you, my lord. 'Tis Miss Theodora. She has taken a turn."

Serenity moaned and clutched Timothy's arm. "Oh, sweet heavens! Do you think the chill from the sleigh accident caused her to sicken?"

Instead of answering her, Timothy ordered, "Ride back and tell Grandfather we are on our way. Jenkins, return us to Cheyney Park without delay."

Serenity bit back her questions that no one could answer as Timothy handed her into the carriage. The door was barely closed behind him before Jenkins was whipping up the horses. She grasped the handhold on the side of the carriage. She had not expected to return to Cheyney Park . . . not like this.

NINETEEN

$\mathcal{T}$he house was preternaturally silent as Serenity handed her soaked bonnet and cloak to Branson. She wondered if all the guests had sought their rooms in the midst of the hubbub of tragedy that had replaced the holiday excitement.

The butler did not meet her eyes as he said, "Lord Brookindale is with Miss Theodora in her rooms, my lord."

"How does she fare?" Serenity asked tremulously, not sure if she wanted to hear the answer. She had been headstrong in her determination to prove to everyone that they had been mistaken about what Theodora should or should not do. As headstrong as Felix, who had let ambition blind him, for she had been unabashedly proud each time Theodora shown that she could do all Serenity had hoped she could.

"I know only the message His Lordship gave me to send after you, Miss Adams. . . ." He gulped. "Miss Loughlin, I mean."

"Do not fret about such things now." Gathering up her damp skirt, she rushed to the stairs as Timothy added something she did not hear to the butler.

By the time she had reached Theodora's door, Timothy had caught up to her. He winced on every step, and she guessed his injured leg was bothering him. She put her hand on his arm in sympathy, and he gave her a stiff smile.

"Do you want me to go in first?" he asked.

"Of course not! This is my fault."

"On that you are completely right," said the earl as he opened the door wider. "The whole of this is your fault, Miss Loughlin."

Tears jeweled his face where his mouth worked with the emotions he was struggling to control. "May I see her, my lord?"

"If you think you can handle what you are about to see."

"Grandfather," Timothy said with the same rigid tone he had used with Felix, shocking her, for he never had shown his grandfather anything but respect and love, "do not treat her cruelly. She has been a victim in this charade, not the perpetrator of it. All she has done is bring you and I and Theodora and even Aunt Ilse closer as a family."

The earl stepped aside to let them enter the dusky room. "So put away that tone that suggests you are about to don your armor and fight for your lady fair."

"Grandfather, about all this—"

"We will speak of this later."

"My lord," Serenity whispered, "may I see Theodora?"

"This way."

She looked back when she heard Branson's voice. Timothy motioned for her to go with his grandfather as he turned to speak with the butler. Not caring what they were discussing, she rushed to Theodora's bed. She frowned when she saw the covers were undisturbed.

"My lord?" she asked, baffled, as she turned to the earl.

Light flared as lamps were lit. In shock, she stared at Lord Brookindale and Nurse and . . . Theodora. All of them were grinning as if they were enjoying the greatest jest.

Serenity knelt by Theodora's chair. "You are not sick?"

"Only if she ate too many cakes at the gathering tonight," replied the earl as he ruffled the little girl's hair.

Looking up at him, Serenity whispered, "But the message . . . It said that—"

"Theodora had taken a turn." The earl laughed. "A turn for the better. Show her, Theodora."

Serenity held her breath, watching as the little girl slowly bent her elbow until she could pull her hand up to her chest and then, as slowly, unbent it. "Oh, sweet heavens! Look at what you can do!"

"I would say that is quite a turn for the better." The earl's belly laugh brought a restrained chuckle from Nurse and a giggle from Theodora. "She is determined to be able to hold one of those ducklings by spring."

Serenity put her head down on the little girl's lap and gave in to the tears that had burned in her eyes since the messenger had reached them on the icy road. Only now did she realize that everything she had considered a disaster was truly good news. She had found her past, and Theodora was growing stronger every day. Timothy's grandfather might be angry with him, but that wound would heal.

Timothy . . .

His broad hand stroked her damp hair, and she raised her face. Taking her hands, he brought her to her feet. Softly he said,

"It seems as if everyone has what they want tonight." His voice grew hard for a moment. "Even my cousin, who has Melanda."

"Yes."

"Everyone but you and me, sweetheart."

Her heart contracted at the longing he put in that single word. "Yes."

"You know that I love you, don't you?"

"Yes."

"So stay here with me."

"I must go home. Father must be half out of his mind with fear for me."

He reached under his coat. "I had thought of that as well, and, from what I had heard of Sir Philip Loughlin, I could not believe he would wait patiently for word about his missing daughter. I had Branson check Felix's room quickly. My cousin was so bold in his plan that he saw no reason to hide his malevolent machinations." He pulled out a slip of paper. "Branson brought me this."

She scanned the letter and gasped. When the earl held out his hand, she gave it to him. He snarled an oath.

"What is it?" Theodora asked, not willing to be left out of the conversation.

"It seems that Felix did not confine his letter-writing enterprise to that single note in Serenity's apron pocket." Timothy's smile grew strained. "He had started a letter to Serenity's father in London to let Sir Philip think that nothing was amiss with his daughter, so Sir Philip would not come seeking her and ruin my cousin's plans for his revenge and obtaining his ambitions for both himself and his father."

"What revenge?" Theodora's eyes gleamed with excitement.

The earl tapped her nose. "You *and* Timothy have been reading too many novels. There is no revenge." His intent gaze warned the rest of them that what he was about to say would be what was shared with the rest of the Polite World. "Felix is simply choosing to try some new things beyond the walls of Cheyney Park."

"Way beyond." Timothy grinned. "In India, to be exact."

"India?" Lord Brookindale's mouth worked as it had by the door, and Serenity realized he was trying not to laugh now, as he had been then. The laugh escaped in an explosion of mirth. "An excellent choice, my boy. Absolutely excellent. Some discipline and appreciation for a Yorkshire winter will be good for him."

Theodora tugged on Serenity's dress. "So are you staying?"

"What are you waiting for, my boy?" grumbled the earl.

"Waiting for?" asked Timothy with a wink at Serenity.

"Ask her to marry you before I ask her myself."

"You would ask her to marry me?"

Grandfather chuckled, sounding so much like Timothy that Serenity wanted to hug them both. "No, you widgeon, I would ask her to marry *me*. I am determined to have such an intelligent lass in this family. Any woman who can see through your cousin and through you and—" he wagged a finger at her—"and almost through me is a prize indeed. So what are you waiting for?"

"I believe I am waiting to decide whether I should ask Serenity or Helen to be my wife."

"Papa would be distressed if you call me anything but Helen when he is about, for I was named for his mother." Serenity's eyes widened as another bit of her past fell into place. "You have to own, Timothy, that things have not been the least bit serene since we began all this."

He folded her hands in his and dropped to one knee. "I believe I shall solve the whole of this by asking you to become Lady Cheyney. Then no one will have a problem in deciding how to address you."

"You will call me Lady Cheyney?"

"I shall call you my beloved wife, if you will only say yes."

She drew one hand out of his and tousled his hair. "Yes," she whispered.

As he stood, Theodora wrinkled her nose. "You are not going to do something disgusting like kiss her, are you?"

"I am afraid so," Timothy replied with a laugh as he gathered Serenity into his arms. His voice lowered to a husky whisper, "Again and again and again."

ABOUT THE AUTHOR

Jo Ann Ferguson is a lifelong storyteller and the author of numerous romantic novels. She also writes as Jo Ann Brown and Mary Jo Kim. A former US Army officer, she has served as the president of the national board of the Romance Writers of America and taught creative writing at Brown University. She currently lives in Nevada with her family, which includes one very spoiled cat.

JO ANN FERGUSON

FROM OPEN ROAD MEDIA

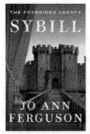

OPEN ROAD

INTEGRATED MEDIA

INTEGRATED MEDIA